W9-ADV-164

Surprising Cecilia

by Susan Gonzales Abraham &
Denise Gonzales Abraham

CINCO PUNTOS PRESS
El Paso, Texas

Surprising Cecilia. Copyright © 2006 by Susan Gonzales Abraham and Denise Gonzales Abraham. All rights reserved. No part of this book may be used or reproduced in any manner whatsoever without written consent from the publisher, except for brief quotations for reviews. For further information, write Cinco Puntos Press, 701 Texas Avenue, El Paso, TX 79901; or call 1-915-838-1625.

FIRST EDITION
10 9 8 7 6 5 4 3 2 1

Library of Congress Cataloging-in-Publication Data

Abraham, Susan Gonzales, 1951-
 Surprising Cecilia / by Susan and Denise Gonzales Abraham.– 1st ed.
   p. cm.
 Summary: In the 1930s as she ventures from her small and poor New Mexican farming community to go to high school in the city, teenaged Cecilia finds herself challenged in unexpected ways.
 ISBN-13: 978-0-938317-96-8
 ISBN-10: 0-938317-96-2
 [1. High schools–Fiction. 2. Mexican Americans–Fiction. 3. Schools–Fiction. 4. Family life–New Mexico–Fiction. 5. Farm life–New Mexico–Fiction. 6. New Mexico–History–20th century–Fiction.] I. Abraham, Denise Gonzales, 1949- II. Title.
 PZ7.A1665Sur 2005
 [Fic]–dc22

                                                    2005013981

Cover art is based on a painting by Gaspar Enriquez
Book and cover design by Paco Casas

R06056 92036

Dedicated to the children of
José and Josefina Gonzales

Elías, Cecilia, Robert, Adolfo,
Celia & Belia

CHILDREN'S DEPARTMENT
WOODSON REGIONAL
9525 S. HALSTED ST. 60628

CHAPTER 1

Hay que bailar al son que le toca.
One must dance to the tune that is played.

The yellow school bus raised a cloud of dust as it bumped and jolted its way along the dry New Mexico road. María Cecilia Gonzales sat staring out the bus window, oblivious to the shouts and yells of the other students. Her pretty cousin Belle sat next to her.

"Why are you so quiet, Cecilia? You haven't said a word since we got on the bus," Belle said.

"I'm afraid if I say anything, I'll wake up and realize this is just a dream, and that Mamá didn't let me go to high school after all," Cecilia said. "*Todavía no lo creo*—I still can't believe it!"

"*Yo tampoco.* I'm so excited I can hardly stand it. *¡Qué emoción!* To think we're actually going to high school. We're really grown up now," Belle said. She wiggled excitedly on the narrow bench and ran her fingers through her curly brown hair. "Don't you just love my new short haircut?" Belle asked. *"Las trenzas son para niñas.* Braids are for little girls. You should cut your hair like mine. *Es muy importante estar de moda.* Don't you want to be modern? How else will we fit in with all the town kids?"

Cecilia just smiled. She loved her own shiny dark braids tied with white velvet ribbons and hanging down her back. True to style, her cousin Belle didn't wait for an answer but chattered on about her hair, her new patent leather pumps, and the store-bought dress her mother had brought back from a shopping trip to El Paso. Cecilia couldn't have squeezed in a word even if she had wanted to.

Belle screamed shrilly in Cecilia's ear as she was hit on the forehead by a spit wad. Cecilia's hand flew to her ear just in time to ward off another spit wad aimed at her head. A paper airplane landed in her lap. She didn't even turn around. Her Apodaca cousins were at it again. Those boys—all ten of them—were always pulling rough pranks and playing mean jokes on people. Five of them were on the bus today, all armed with slingshots they had carved just for this occasion—the first day of school. Cecilia didn't have time to bother with childish games. She was on her way to high school!

"These stupid boys. They're nothing but *campesinos.* Farm boys," Belle said with disdain. "We're going to be in school with real town boys," she said. "I can't wait!"

"Well, we're farm girls, but at least we know how to

behave. Elías is always a gentleman. *Es un caballero.* Mamá is always so proud of him," Cecilia said, noticing that her brother wasn't throwing paper like their cousins, but sat quietly looking out the bus window. She knew he would much rather be back home working on the farm with Papá.

A spit wad flew over them and hit Cecilia's head. Belle turned to face the delinquent boys saying angrily, "If you don't stop, I'm going to tell your mother! You should be ashamed of yourselves! *¡Le voy a decir a mi Tía Teotiste!*"

"Tattletale!" one of them yelled at her. Another spit wad whizzed by.

"¡Qué importa, no nos hace nada!" another one shouted. "Our mother won't do anything to us!"

"¡Salvajes!" she yelled back. "You're nothing but a bunch of savages!" She turned back to Cecilia with an angry gleam in her dark brown eyes. "Our Tía would whip their legs with the *chicote* if she knew how they are behaving! They'd pay attention to the leather strap, that's for sure!"

Cecilia just laughed, brushed the paper from her lap, and smoothed her hair behind her ear. She had taken great care this morning to look her best. Today was one of the most important days of her life. She had been dreaming for years of going to high school, and now her dream had come true. She had struggled so hard to get to this point. All last year, Cecilia's mother had threatened to keep her home after the eighth grade. Mamá felt a young girl should stay home and wait to be married while she learned how to cook and run a household. She didn't understand how important an education was to her daughter. Only this morning they had had the same old argument.

"Your time would be better spent helping me here in the house," Mamá had chided Cecilia as she got ready for school. "And Elías should be helping his father with the chile harvest instead of the two of you running off to school. Your brother is already a good farmer, and you will be a good farmer's wife someday. I want to be proud of you on the day you marry and set up your own household. I want people to see that I taught my daughter well."

"*Por favor, Mamá*. Please try to understand me," Cecilia had pleaded. "I love to go to school. I want to learn everything I can. I will help you when I get home. I promise I will get all my work done. I promise my school work won't interfere with my chores."

As usual Mamá had turned away, banging pans and muttering under her breath in anger and annoyance. Her oldest daughter would always be a puzzle to her.

Another obstacle standing between Cecilia and high school had been her brother Elías, who wasn't as interested in school as she was. Elías was an indifferent student and had failed the high school entrance exam. Mamá had declared that Cecilia could not go to high school unless Elías went, too. Through the kind intervention of their teacher, Miss May Malone, Elías was able to take and pass a makeup test. To Cecilia, it was a miracle. But her beloved Tía Sara knew better.

"Entre lo dicho y lo hecho hay un gran trecho," she said. She knew some things are easier said than done. She knew of the late nights Cecilia had spent tutoring her brother, and in turn how hard he had studied and struggled to pass the difficult exam. But she also knew her niece and nephew were made of hardy stuff and could accomplish anything they chose. To Tía Sara it came as no surprise that both Cecilia and Elías were now entering their first year at Hatch Union High School.

Cecilia had tried to hide her excitement all morning. She forced herself to behave as normally as possible, even though her stomach felt like a clenched fist, and her heart was thumping loudly in her chest. She had risen early to do her daily chores—make the beds, dress her little sister Sylvia, set the large kitchen table for breakfast, pour milk for her brothers and sisters, and wash and dry all the breakfast dishes—before she could spare some time to dress with extra care for school. She knew Mamá would be annoyed if she suspected Cecilia was shirking her duties or paying too much attention to her appearance. It would be disastrous if Mamá caught her looking at herself in the mirror. Why, she might even forbid Cecilia to go to school! Cecilia could hardly bear to think of it—not after all her hard-won happiness. So she had gone about her routine methodically, as though nothing was special about this day.

But this day *was* special. Not only would Cecilia be starting high school, but she would also be seeing Johnny Tafoya again. Cecilia and Johnny had a special relationship. They had known each other all their lives and had grown up on neighboring farms in the Rio Grande valley of New Mexico. Sharing a love of reading and learning, they had been the brightest students in their class. At the end of the last school year, Johnny had given Cecilia a special valentine, and—to her amazement—a kiss on her cheek! She had hoped they would see each other often over the long summer vacation to read together from the high school reading list. She had hoped that he would kiss her again.

Cecilia looked out the bus window without really seeing the green fields and the purple mountains in the distance. She daydreamed about Johnny and the last time she had seen him on a beautiful warm day in June. He had ridden over on his horse Chispa to visit his friend Elías, but Cecilia knew he had really come to see her. The three of them had walked out to the fruit orchards, Johnny's horse obediently following behind. Elías had left them alone while he went to the stable to get his own horse Panky. Cecilia and Johnny had sat in the shade of a leafy pear tree. How handsome Johnny looked! Cecilia felt breathless and dizzy, and her heart was racing as Johnny took her hand in his.

"I really came over to see *you*," Johnny admitted. "I wanted you to know that I won't be able to see you this summer like we planned. My grandmother is sick in El Paso. My mother is taking my sister and me to stay with her for the summer, but I don't want to go!" Johnny squeezed Cecilia's hand tighter.

"I'm sorry about your grandmother," Cecilia said. She tried to hide her deep disappointment as she looked into his eyes. "I don't want you to go either," she said almost in a whisper. And she choked back her tears, trying not to let Johnny see just how much she cared.

"I can't wait until I'm old enough to do what I want," Johnny said angrily as he threw a rock at a shriveled brown pear that lay on the ground. "I'll miss you, Cecilia, but I promise I will write to you. Will you write me back?"

"Oh, yes! *Seguro*. Of course, I will!" Cecilia said. "I promise!"

And before Elías came riding up on Panky, Johnny had leaned over and kissed Cecilia on the lips under the pear tree. Her first real kiss! Her heart had felt as if it would explode, and she could hardly breathe. She would remember that moment forever. Now she put her finger to her lips, remembering the feel of his warm lips on her own. Her first kiss, and Johnny had given it to her!

All summer Cecilia had waited for a letter from Johnny. The mail came to the nearby general mercantile store owned by Cecilia's Tío Ben and Tía María. Tía María sorted the mail and stuck the envelopes into little wooden pigeonholes behind the counter. Every day Cecilia would find some excuse to walk to the store—to visit Belle or to carry a message from her mother to her uncle and aunt or to make a small purchase. She would crane her neck to see if the box labeled "José Gonzales" contained an envelope, and every day she had been disappointed. But each time she was also

15

a little relieved because Mamá would have been angry if Cecilia had received a letter from a boy without her permission. And surely Tía María would tell Mamá the minute a letter came for Cecilia all the way from El Paso. Mamá would demand to know who it was from and what was in it.

Cecilia had agonized all summer about Johnny's broken promise. *He said he would write me. He made me promise to write him back. Why hasn't he written me a letter? What could have happened?* All these thoughts ran through her mind over and over again. At night she would lie awake in the small iron bed she shared with her younger sister Belia and stare at the gauzy curtains that fluttered in the warm breeze that wafted through the open window. Her stomach would tighten and her heart would pound as she thought of Johnny and the kiss he had given her. Why hadn't he written? Had he changed his mind about her? Had he met another girl in the city? Had he forgotten all about her? And Cecilia would bury her head in her pillow and cry herself to sleep.

Now, today, Cecilia felt excited and nervous about seeing Johnny again. Surely he would have a good explanation about why he never wrote to her. Maybe his mother wouldn't give him a stamp for the envelope. Maybe his grandmother had been so ill he didn't have time to write a letter. He would explain it all, and she would accept his explanation. Together they would find their classrooms—maybe Johnny would even carry her books for her. Everyone would see them and know they were a couple. Cecilia sighed. *¡Qué romántico!*

Another spit wad hit her on the shoulder and fell on her lap. As she brushed it away, she smoothed the skirt of the new dress that Mamá had ordered for her from the Sears catalog. This dress was different from the ones she had worn last year. It was dark blue cotton with buttons all the way from the white piqué collar down to the mid-calf hem. A blue patent leather belt cinched her small waist and made her feel very grown up. Last year all her dresses had drop waists and broad sailor collars. If only her new black pumps had arrived in time from the mail-order catalog!

Cecilia frowned as she caught a glimpse of the rough brown boots that she tried to keep hidden under the seat. They weren't her boots at all. They were an old pair Elías had outgrown. But when Cecilia's shoes hadn't arrived in time for the first day of school, she had no other shoes to wear. Her younger sister Belia was already wearing Cecilia's own outgrown ones. Mamá, tired and red-faced from the heat of the kitchen wood stove, had said crossly, *"Ponte los zapatos de tu hermano.* You can wear your brother's old shoes. You're going to school to study, not to look like a movie star." Cecilia was afraid to complain lest Mamá change her mind about letting her go to school.

"Más vale algo que nada, sobrinita," said Tía Sara to her niece. "Better to have something than nothing." Tía Sara always had a *dicho*, or proverb, on the tip of her tongue for any occasion. It was her way of instructing her nieces and nephews in the ways of the world and of sharing the wis-

dom of past generations. *"Cuando no hay remedio, hay que adaptarse.* We have to make do with what we have. Roberto's new boots were too tight, so we had to stretch them with corn." Roberto had filled his boots with dry corn and then poured water into them. The corn absorbed the water and swelled, stretching the leather just enough for the mail-order boots to fit more comfortably.

"Be thankful you have any shoes to wear at all. The Navarro children go to school barefoot," Mamá said with a finality that warned Cecilia to keep quiet.

Cecilia held back the tears that stung behind her deep brown eyes and reluctantly laced up the heavy, scuffed farm boots. She and Belia often wore their brothers' old boots when doing outdoor chores to protect their own shoes from the mud and muck of the farm. Other farm girls did the same. It wouldn't be so bad. After all, she was going to school with her friends and neighbors—children she had grown up with and known all her life. Taking a deep breath, she tried to calm her nerves and tune out the rowdy din of the school bus.

How wonderful and miraculous to be going to high school at last! Cecilia had thought of nothing else for the past year. This would be the start of a new life. She was on her way to achieving her dream of graduating from high school and going to work in a big city like El Paso. She would learn to type and take shorthand and improve her English skills. Then she could get a good job and earn real money so that she could help Papá pay the mortgage on the farm. She would be able to send money home every week to help Mamá buy shoes and clothes for her younger brothers, Fito and Roberto, and her little sisters, Belia and Sylvia. Even Mamá and Tía Sara, who were so self-sacrificing in their care of the family, would get treats now and then—maybe a new lace *mantilla* for mass or fancy chocolates in a silver foil box. Oh, anything was possible once she had an education and a job!

The bus screeched to a halt in front of a large white building. It wasn't made of adobe like her little elementary school, but was constructed like a modern building with white plaster walls and an ornate gable over the main entrance. Tall glass windows with real screens could be opened during hot weather without admitting hundreds of pesky gnats and flies that buzzed and stung and made it hard to concentrate on what the teacher was saying. Cecilia had heard the school even had gas heating in the winter. No one had to get there early to start the wood stove or stay late to clean out the ashes. No one had to bring in pails of water every day for the students to drink out of a dipper. The high school had water fountains. When she was thirsty, all she would have to do was bend over a spout and turn a knob. She had also heard that not only was there a real restroom instead of an outhouse, but there was one just for the girls and one just for the boys. Amazing! And to think she would be spending the next four years in this wonderful place. She felt like the luckiest girl in the world!

Cecilia and Belle waited for the rowdy boys to leave the bus before they stepped down onto the concrete sidewalk. Cecilia stood rooted for a moment with surprise and shyness when she saw dozens of students milling about the front entrance to the school. Groups of boys and girls sat on benches or under the trees talking and laughing. Everyone seemed to know each other. The students looked different somehow. A lot of them had blonde hair. And the girls—most of them had short hair, like Belle's. Suddenly she felt self-conscious about her long braids. And she hadn't realized there would be so many students here! She clung to Belle's arm.

"Let go of my arm!" Belle whispered angrily. "You're making us look like scared farm girls." And she flounced off to say hello to Geraldine Dickerson, the daughter of a local grocer whom she had met during the summer. Belle's own father, Cecilia's Tío Ben, owned the general mercantile store in their home village of Derry. Belle's father always had business in Hatch, and Belle and her younger sister Clory often accompanied him. Belle felt much more comfortable meeting new people and being in the larger town than Cecilia did. Cecilia stood unsure of where to go, looking around for a familiar face. She saw no one she recognized. Where were Nestora and Virginia? And where was Johnny? She noticed a group of boys from her town slouching under a tree. Johnny should have been with them. Why wasn't he there? Her heart was pounding like a hammer in her chest. Unsure of what to do, she started to walk hesitantly toward the large main doors of the school.

"Cecilia! Cecilia! Wait for me!" someone shouted.

Cecilia saw her best friend Virginia and let out a deep

sigh of relief. She hadn't realized she had been holding her breath. At last—a familiar face! Virginia ran up to her, and the girls hugged. A sweet-faced girl, Virginia wore her shiny brown hair long and loose, clipped back from her brow by a tortoise-shell barrette.

"Why weren't you on the bus today?" Cecilia asked her. "The bus stops at your farm first."

"Papá had business in Hatch, so he drove me in. What was the bus like?" Virginia asked.

"Very bumpy and noisy. You know how the Apodacas are. And we have to get up earlier than last year to catch it. But I guess it's better than walking. I'm so glad to see you! Belle left, and I felt like everyone was staring at me," Cecilia said.

"Well, they are! You're wearing farm boots with that pretty new dress!" Virginia said. *"¿Qué pasó?"*

"Oh, Virginia! My new pumps didn't come in. I didn't have any other shoes to wear. I'm so embarrassed. But how could I miss the first day of school?" Cecilia's face felt hot, and she knew it must be red from the shame she felt. *"¡Ay, qué vergüenza!"*

"It doesn't matter. Your shoes will come in, and then no one will even remember this," Virginia said, trying to comfort her. "Everyone is too excited to pay much attention anyway."

If only that were true! As Cecilia and Virginia walked up the main stairs, Cecilia noticed more than a few pairs of eyes on her boots, and she was sure she heard whispers and giggles as she passed some of the other girls. They were all wearing pumps with the ankle straps that were in fashion now along with cotton stockings. She wanted to dig a hole and crawl in! Fighting the urge to turn and run back home, Cecilia walked into the building to look for her first-period class. She didn't want to make matters worse by being late to class the first day of school!

"Aquí está. Here's our English class," said Virginia, and she pulled Cecilia into a large white room filled with modern wooden desks and a large chalkboard that took up one entire wall. A bulletin board was filled with notices and posters announcing club meetings and other activities open to the students. The wooden floor had been waxed till it shone. Everything was so different from her elementary school in Derry. This room was beautiful and modern. Once again, Cecilia felt excited to be there and forgot all about her shoes.

All morning Cecilia went from class to class, wide-eyed with amazement. So this was high school! She had a different room and a different teacher every period. Last year, all the students had been in one room with Miss Malone teaching all subjects. This school not only had many different classrooms, but it also had a gymnasium, an auditorium with a stage, an agriculture shop, a study hall, and even a sewing room and a kitchen for the home economics girls.

But best of all was the library! Cecilia could hardly believe her eyes. Shelves filled with books lined every wall. Shelves filled with books stood in the middle of the room. There were books everywhere! There was even a magazine rack filled with shiny new magazines. No longer would she have to beg her eccentric Tía María for permission to read her hoard of magazines inside a hot storage shed. No longer would she have to turn pages with fingers frozen numb from the cold after cleaning her aunt's house in the winter.

She could read all the magazines and books she wanted during her study hall period. And just imagine! She could actually check them out and take them home to read late at night after all her chores were done. *This is paradise,* Cecilia thought.

The wonders of the library took Cecilia's mind off the nervousness and embarrassment she had felt that morning. But one puzzle still nagged at her. Where was Johnny Tafoya? This summer she had looked forward to seeing him when school started, but she hadn't seen him all morning. He wasn't in any of her classes—most of the twenty-five freshmen were together in math and English. He should have been there, too. *Could he be sick?* Cecilia wondered. *I'll write down all the assignments for him so he can make up the work,* she thought. *Por supuesto vendrá mañana. I'm sure he'll be here tomorrow.* She remembered her shoes. Maybe it was better Johnny wasn't at school today to see her wearing farm boots with her new school dress. Maybe his family was late coming back from El Paso. Maybe her new shoes would arrive in today's mail, and he would never know of her embarrassment.

Rrrrring! Rrrrring! The lunch bell startled Cecilia out of her reverie. The morning had passed so quickly. Her head was spinning from all the new things she had seen and heard.

23

"Let's eat our burritos outside under a tree," said Virginia. "All the kids meet out in front during lunch."

As the two girls made their way down a crowded noisy hall, Cecilia realized that every boy or girl who passed them looked down at her boots. She wasn't imagining it. Groups of students were snickering and pointing as she passed.

"No! I'm sorry. I feel sick. Go find Belle and eat with her. I don't want to eat outside!" Cecilia cried. She couldn't bear the thought of sitting in the schoolyard with all the other students gawking and laughing at her. How humiliating! She ran into the girls' restroom and locked herself inside a stall. No one could see her now. She leaned her head against the door and began to cry. Why hadn't her shoes come in time? Why did it have to happen to her? Why couldn't Papá and Mamá afford a second pair of shoes for her? All the joy she had felt in her new dress had been replaced by the shame and embarrassment of her shoes.

"When I grow up and get a job, I'll buy myself all the shoes I want," she promised herself. "But how can I go out there again wearing these ugly old boots? And what if my shoes don't come in for weeks? What will I do? What will I do?" she cried. *"¡Ay qué vergüenza!* How embarrassing!" Alone in the restroom, she began to cry even harder until her sobs turned into hiccups. How would she ever get through this day?

Cecilia's lunch sat uneaten in its small basket. Mamá had fixed all her children *burritos de papas y asadero.* Cecilia normally loved potato and cheese burritos, but now she couldn't swallow even one bite. She was too miserable to eat. She felt no hunger—only shame and disillusionment. Elías would eat her burrito on the bus ride home. He was always hungry. That way Mamá would never know she hadn't eaten her lunch and start asking prying questions. Cecilia just couldn't let Mamá know what had happened today; she couldn't tell her about the shame and misery she had felt. Mamá would only say, *"¿No te dije?* Didn't I tell you nothing good will come from your going to school and wanting more than we can provide?" She might even forbid Cecilia to go back to school. Cecilia gritted her teeth at the thought of having to give up her dream. But most important, Cecilia didn't want Mamá to feel she and Papá had failed her in any way. She could handle her embarrassment, and she would do anything to protect her parents from feeling it, too. She would rather die than see the hurt in their eyes if they thought Cecilia was ashamed of her family.

The bell signaling the end of lunch rang too soon. *"¡Ay Dios! ¿Qué haré?* What shall I do? I must look terrible! How can I go to class?" she cried. Cecilia left the stall, sobs catching in her throat. Hiccupping, she looked at herself in the mirror. The girl who looked back at her had teary swollen eyes and a splotchy red face. She looked as bad as she felt. Quickly, Cecilia turned on the faucet and splashed cool water on her hot face. She smoothed back the loose ends of her hair from her forehead with her damp hands. There was nothing more she could do. She would just have to go back into the hall and face everyone.

Walking out the door was one of the hardest things Cecilia had ever done. She made her way to her next class, eyes straight ahead. The soft clump of her boots as she walked sounded like an entire marching army to her ears.

"Just keep walking," she told herself. "Just keep walking."

When the last bell rang at three o'clock, Cecilia headed straight for the bus. Once seated, she again hid her feet beneath the seat. Virginia came to sit with her. She could tell that Cecilia was still upset.

"*Ay, amiga,* if I had an extra pair of shoes I would give them to you," she said. "But I'm wearing the only pair I have. These are the ones I wore all last year. Remember? They pinch my toes, but there's no money for new shoes right now."

Cecilia knew Virginia's family had the same money troubles as her own. Her friend's genuine concern touched her deeply, and she felt ashamed of herself. She at least would be getting new shoes any day in the mail. Poor Virginia might be forced to wear shoes that were too tight, perhaps for the rest of the year. And if her family couldn't afford new shoes this year after all, Virginia's father would have to cut the leather toes off her shoes so they wouldn't hurt. She put an arm around Virginia's shoulder and gave her a hug.

"*Gracias, amiga.* I know you would help if you could. And I'm sorry I ran off and didn't eat lunch with you. I promise we'll eat together tomorrow." Cecilia said. Then she blurted out the question she had been wanting to ask all day.

"Virginia, I noticed Johnny Tafoya wasn't at school today.

Do you know why?" she asked.

"*Sí, sí.* Didn't you hear? He and his mother are staying in El Paso. His grandmother is still too sick to be alone. And Johnny's parents want him to go to high school in El Paso," Virginia said.

Cecilia fought hard not to show her bitter disappointment. She bit her lip and turned her face toward the window. But her heart felt as though it had fallen into her stomach. Even the treasures of the school library couldn't make up for Johnny's absence. She had had such hopes for their friendship. All summer she had dreamed that he would ask her to be his girlfriend. After all, he had given her that special valentine last year and even kissed her on the last day of school and under the pear tree. She had fantasized about Johnny holding her hand, eating lunch with her under a shady cottonwood tree in front of the school, the two of them pouring over a book, heads touching as they studied together. Now the pretty pictures she had created in her mind were broken and scattered like dry, brittle leaves in the wind.

Could the day get any worse? Cecilia thought. *Why am I such a dreamer?* she asked herself. *I built this day up in my mind, and everything has gone wrong. Why can't I be more realistic, like Mamá?* She felt tears well up in her eyes again. "*Ya me cansé. I'm tired of crying. I will NOT cry anymore!*" she told herself.

As the bus bumped its way down the rough country road, jolting as it stopped to let students off, jerking to a start once again, the boys in the back began to yell and throw paper as they had in the morning. Their shouts and rough play gave Cecilia a headache. How could she think with all this noise around her? She actually began to miss the long walk she had made every day the past eight years from her farm to the one-room schoolhouse in Derry. During those walks, she had been able to gather her thoughts and plan her goals and dream of her future.

"And I miss Miss Malone. She's the best teacher I ever had. Now I have five different teachers. Everything is so strange. And I hardly know any of the students in my classes. And they laughed at me! And I HATE these boots!" she screamed inside her head. "I will NOT cry, I will NOT cry," she repeated under her breath. She couldn't risk the other students on the bus, especially her Apodaca cousins, seeing her red-faced and crying like a child. She was grown up now, and she would have to face up to her disappointments. It was time to stop crying and start dealing with the frustrations of life. She could almost hear Tía Sara's soft voice saying, *"Hay que bailar al son que le toca."* One must dance to the tune that is played. Tía Sara was right, as usual. She would just have to make do, that's all.

Cecilia felt the heavy weight of the books resting in her lap. Her teachers had already assigned pages and pages of homework. Cecilia sighed. *How can I read and outline all these pages and work all these math problems and still finish all my work at home?* She was genuinely worried. Mamá resented the hours Cecilia spent reading and studying. Mamá expected her to help prepare supper and do most of the cleaning up afterwards. She also had to help put the younger children to bed. And then

Mamá might ask her to mop the kitchen floor or to clean the glass chimneys of the kerosene lamps they used for light after dark. Or she might have to shuck corn or shell peas for tomorrow's supper. It took a lot of shelling to fill up a pot with enough peas to feed her family of nine—Papá, Mamá, Tía Sara, Elías, Fito, Belia, Roberto, Sylvia, and Cecilia herself. As the oldest daughter, all these household chores fell on her. By the time she finished, she would be exhausted and sleepy. But she would still have several hours of homework to do.

"Ay Virgencita, ayúdame, por favor," she prayed, whispering against the glass windowpane. "Sweet Virgin, please help me get through this school year and pass all my classes. Please let Mamá understand how important it is for me to have time to study and do my homework. Please don't let her change her mind and make me stay home. *Te lo ruego,"* she begged. *And please let me get a letter from Johnny.* A sob caught in her throat.

The old bus rattled to a stop in front of the general mercantile store owned by Tío Ben and his wife, Tía María. All the students who lived in that area got off the bus, including Cecilia, Elías, and their cousin Belle, who lived with her parents and her sister Clory behind the store.

"Hasta mañana," Cecilia told Virginia.

"See you tomorrow. It will be better, you'll see," Virginia said. Cecilia certainly hoped so. How could it be worse? At least she had stopped crying and could face Mamá and Tía Sara with dry eyes and a smile. Tía Sara would want to know all about her day. Cecilia could hardly wait to tell her about the library and all the books she had seen there. She hoped Mamá would be interested in it, too.

"I'm going to the fields to help Papá," Elías said. Free from the confines of the schoolroom and the bus, he ran blissfully and lightheartedly to find his father. Elías had the same homework as Cecilia, but she knew he, like most of the other farm boys, wouldn't do it. They had too much work to do on the family farms. And besides, Elías *wanted* to be a farmer. Cecilia knew he was going to high school so that she could go, too. She knew his heart wasn't really in it as hers was. But whether he went to school or not, Cecilia adored her older brother.

"Well, no sense wasting time. I'd better go inside and start my chores so I'll have more time to do my homework," she said aloud as she stood on the long, deep porch that ran the length of her adobe home.

Mamá met Cecilia at the screen door of the kitchen. *"Cecilia, ven adentro, mi hija. Tengo algo que decirte.* I need to talk to you," Mamá said. Cecilia was puzzled. Always busy in the kitchen, Mamá never met her at the door like this. And why did Mamá have such a serious look on her face? What could have happened now? Was the bank threatening to foreclose on the farm again? Was Mamá going to tell her she had changed her mind, and Cecilia would not be able to stay in school after all?

"Cecilia, I have something to tell you. *Mi hija*, I'm going to need your help around the house more than ever now. You see, I'm going to have another baby," Mamá said.

And Cecilia burst into tears.

CHAPTER 2

Tras la tempestad viene la calma.
After the storm comes the calm.

H*oy haremos chicos,"* Mamá announced at the breakfast table on Friday morning. *"Hijos,* you need to pick *elotes* for me this morning before you run off to school."

"Yippeee!" shouted Roberto. "I love *chicos!"*

"A mí también me gustan mucho," said Fito. "I'll race you to the cornfield." He and Roberto jumped from their seats, almost knocking over their chairs, and ran out the door. They would spend the next half hour filling baskets with the last corn of the season—big, overgrown yellow ears—so Mamá could make the delicious corn dish known as *chicos.* Mamá frowned as the screen door slammed shut behind them.

"¡Esos muchachitos traviesos!" she said as she rose slowly from the table. *"Me ponen nerviosa.* Those boys are get-

ting on my nerves." Mamá's face already showed signs of exhaustion, and it was still early in the morning. Cecilia jumped up from the table to start clearing away the breakfast dishes.

"Mamá, siéntese y descanse. Sit down and have another cup of coffee. I'll wash the dishes," she told her mother. Mamá sat back down with a sigh.

"Ay, Señor, I'm so tired lately. It was easier to carry a baby when I was younger," she said as she poured herself a cup of hot, fragrant coffee.

"Sí, hermana. Tienes que descansar mucho. You need more rest. Let Cecilia and me handle the *chicos* today and tomorrow," said Tía Sara. "After all, tomorrow is Saturday, and Cecilia will not have to go to school." Sara's face clouded with worry as she looked at her sister. Mamá felt more uncomfortable with this pregnancy than with her others. Her back hurt constantly and by the end of every day, her face was pale and wan from exhaustion.

Cecilia noticed her aunt's worried frown. She too realized Mamá was having a difficult time carrying this new baby. She had been helping as much as she could without being asked. Cecilia grabbed a pail and rushed outside to the pump to get water to wash the dishes. She set the bucket under the spout and pumped the long handle vigorously up and down until water began to flow. Carefully she carried the full pail back into the house, set it on the burner of the wood stove, and waited for it to heat. While the water was heating, she gathered all the dirty breakfast dishes and scraped the leftovers into a pail of slops for the pigs. While Tía Sara and Mamá finished their second cups of coffee, Cecilia wiped the table and swept the crumbs from the floor. Keeping the kitchen immaculately clean was a necessity to keep from attracting rodents and insects. Besides, Mamá demanded that all her children keep the large house clean and tidy at all times.

Once the water was hot, Cecilia poured it into a basin with soap and began to wash the dishes. Her face was damp with sweat from the heat of the kitchen stove and the steam of the hot water. She scrubbed plates as fast as she could so she wouldn't be late for the school bus. If she missed the bus, she would have to stay home. Hatch was too far away for her to walk to school. And if she missed school, she wouldn't have her assignments for the weekend. Quickly, she dried and put away the last of the dishes. She grabbed her lunch basket and her books, kissed Mamá and Tía Sara on the cheeks, and rushed to the road in front of her house. Elías, tall and lanky, came running from the barn.

"Do you have my lunch?" he asked.

"*Claro. Lo hice yo misma.* I made it myself—bread, cheese, and an apple," Cecilia said. "*¿Pero dónde está tu tarea?* Where is your English notebook? We had homework last night."

"*No lo hice.* I didn't have time to do it. I had to fix Panky's bridle," he said.

Cecilia sighed. Her brother would never change. He would

always be riding his horse or working on the farm instead of doing his schoolwork. She looked anxiously down the road and saw a cloud of dust in the distance signaling the approach of the bus. Belle came running out of the store next door to Cecilia's farm to wait with her cousins.

"*Hola, primos.* Cecilia, you look so much better with Tía Sara's shoes. But we need to do something about your hair," she said, looking her cousin over. Cecilia was wearing the same dark blue dress she had worn every day this week. Mamá had ordered three new dresses for Cecilia at the cost of three for a dollar from a catalog, and Cecilia would alternate a different one every week.

Cecilia looked down at her shoes. They were Tía Sara's dressy shoes she wore only to *misa* and for festive occasions. Looking at them, Cecilia once again felt a great wave of love for her aunt. It seemed as if Tía Sara was always making sacrifices for Cecilia and her family. When Cecilia had burst into tears last Monday and had been inconsolable, Tía Sara knew something was wrong. She knew Cecilia better than anyone and suspected that something besides Mamá's pregnancy was upsetting Cecilia.

"*¿Qué te pasa, sobrinita?* What is wrong? Tell me, please," she told Cecilia gently as Cecilia lay sobbing on her bed.

"*¡Ay, Tía!* I know you are always saying, '*más vale pan duro que ninguno,*' but they laughed at me. I tried not to care, but I was so embarrassed. I didn't know what to do. I hid in the restroom. It was my shoes!" she managed to say between her sobs.

Tía Sara quietly left the room and came back carrying her soft white leather pumps with a bow on the strap.

"*Aquí te presto mis zapatos,* Cecilia. You may borrow my shoes until yours come in the mail," she said.

"No, no, Tía! Those are your best shoes. I don't want to get them dirty and scuffed," Cecilia said.

"*Insisto. Haz lo que te pido.* Please do as I ask. These shoes are going to waste in the closet. I want you to wear them. Please do it for me," Tía Sara said. Cecilia had thrown her arms around her aunt's neck and kissed her cheek.

"*Gracias, Tía.* When I get a job, I'm going to buy you a beautiful outfit with matching shoes!" she promised.

Tía Sara laughed. "*Abrazos y besos no rompen huesos,*" she said. "Your kisses and hugs are enough for me."

The shoes were pretty and went well with the white collar of her dress. They were a little too big for Cecilia, so she had to stuff the toes with paper. But a little discomfort was far superior to wearing her brother's farm boots! She followed Belle and Elías eagerly onto the school bus.

By the end of the week, Cecilia had become more accustomed to her new routine at school and to the new situation at home. Another baby coming! And Sylvia barely out of diapers! Cecilia had recovered from her emotional reaction to Mamá's news. She had been so tired and disappointed her first day in high school, that's all. She knew things would get better, just as Virginia had predicted. But another baby! More diapers, more work. More crying, less sleep. But also more giggles, more smiles, more love. Cecilia could already smell the new baby smell of sweet milk and rose-scented soap. She could almost feel the soft, warm body nestled in her arms. Maybe it *was* time for another baby in the house—another little being to sleep in the crib that Sylvia had outgrown.

Cecilia was looking forward to school today. She had decided to not let Johnny's absence bother her, but just thinking about his warm smile made her heart ache. She pushed thoughts of Johnny to the back of her mind and thought about her classes. One of her favorites was home economics. She was learning such interesting things. This week, Miss Gustafson was teaching the class all about fabric—its colors and textures. Today they would be selecting patterns and fabric to begin their sewing project for the semester. Cecilia could hardly wait to use the modern sewing machines in the classroom. At home, Mamá wouldn't allow her to use the old Montgomery Ward pedal sewing machine that sat in a corner of the dining room. Tía Sara did all the sewing and mending for the household on that machine, and it was too valuable to risk letting Cecilia or the other children use it and possibly break it.

Cecilia entered her home economics sewing room with anticipation. Most of the freshmen girls were in this class. Belle was there, and Nestora, and Virginia, and many town girls who Cecilia hadn't really gotten to know yet. She discovered she was very shy and embarrassed around them. They seemed so sophisticated and at ease with everything, while she still walked around in a state of amazement. The town girls weren't unfriendly or anything like that—they were just so different. Many of them had pale skin and blonde hair. They weren't tanned and dark like most of the farm girls. Cecilia was glad Mamá always made her wear a sunbonnet when she worked in the garden. She heard them talk about buying their clothes at Peacock's Clothing Store in Hatch and going on shopping trips all the way to El Paso. Unlike her, they wore different dresses every day. They even spoke differently, using words like "swell" and "snazzy" and calling each other "kiddo." Even Belle had nonchalantly remarked this morning that Alonzo Hatch had a "snazzy" car, and she would give anything to ride in it. And they all wore their hair in a chin-length bob, either straight or in curls. Most of them had bangs, too. Even Nestora went home after the first day and had her mother cut off ten inches of hair! Virginia vowed that she would cut hers off this weekend once she had convinced her mother. Cecilia wondered, *What would Mamá say if I cut my hair? If I ask her, I know she will say no. Do I dare cut it without her permission? Belle thinks I should, but I'm not like Belle. And if I did, would Mamá ever feel she could trust me again?* Cecilia felt guilt at the thought of giving Mamá another problem during her pregnancy.

Inside the sewing room, Miss Gustafson was handing out bolts of cloth to the girls who were squealing with delight and excitement. Fabric of all colors and shades covered the tables—yards and yards of forest green, pale yellow, sky blue, deep brown, cool lavender, bright red, even simple black. The girls stood around holding up fabric to their faces or wrapping it around their waists and looking at themselves in the long mirrors that lined one wall. Cecilia picked up a bolt of white material covered with clusters of red cherries. It reminded her of the kitchen at home. Mamá loved cherries and had glued cherry decals on all the white cabinet doors. *"I don't think I want a dress made out of this!"* she thought.

"Girls! Settle down, please," said Miss Gustafson. She was a tall, thin young woman with a halo of bright yellow hair around her face. Cecilia thought she was beautiful. She had never seen hair that golden except in a picture book. And Miss Gustafson was so kind and patient. From the first day, she had treated all the girls alike, not favoring either the farm girls or the town girls. She did know Belle better than the rest as she was renting a room from Tío Ben and Tía María. Many of the town's teachers boarded with the local families.

The girls came to order, and Miss Gustafson began to discuss the merits of this fabric over that one and which colors would complement each girl best.

"Juanita, this green will bring out the hazel color of your eyes," she said. "And Loretta, I think the darker green will be lovely with your blonde hair." One by one she chose a fabric that best suited each girl. For Belle it was the bright blue, and for Virginia, the pale rose. "Look at Nestora's olive skin. Isn't it rich and beautiful?" Nestora was thrilled with pink, her favorite color. Miss Gustafson made every girl feel special and pretty.

"Cecilia, you're next," she said as she sorted through the bolts of fabric. She held bolt after bolt against Cecilia's face. Cecilia was nervous standing in front of the others while Miss Gustafson studied her face and considered the effect each color had on Cecilia's skin tone. Cecilia's fair face was framed with dark brown hair. Her large eyes were deep-set and dark brown like her hair. Today her cheeks were pink from the warmth of the room and the stares of all the other girls. She felt thin and gawky, and her braids seemed heavy and hot. She bit her lip nervously.

Finally Miss Gustafson said, "Well! Beautiful Cecilia! Cecilia is one of those lucky girls who can wear any color. Take your pick, Cecilia."

Cecilia could have hugged Miss Gustafson right then and there! No one had ever complimented her like that before. She felt her face get even redder. She looked around and saw the other girls smiling and nodding. She smiled back shyly and then reached for the bolt of fabric she had coveted from the very beginning. The material was a soft, azure color that reminded Cecilia of an early spring sky over her beloved farm. It would make a beautiful dress. She clutched the bolt to her chest and went back to her seat.

"*¡Qué suerte tienes!* You're so lucky. Miss Gustafson is right. Every color looks good on you," Belle said grudgingly. Usually it was Belle who got all the attention with her pretty face and vivacious personality. But Cecilia didn't really hear her. She was thinking about Johnny and wondering if he would ever see her in the azure dress.

ON THE BUS that afternoon Belle told Cecilia, "We need to get rid of those braids. Let me cut your hair like mine. I watched the beautician in Hatch when she cut my hair, and I know I can do it. *Ándale, prima.* Don't you feel out of place?"

"I don't know. I think Mamá would be very angry if I did it. I have to think about it," Cecilia said.

"Well, it's always easier to beg forgiveness than to ask permission," Belle countered. "That's how *I* always get what I want."

Cecilia could imagine herself going to confession with Padre Arteta at the Iglesia de San Isidro and begging forgiveness for having disobeyed her mother. Just thinking about kneeling to pray all the Our Fathers he would assign as penance made her knees hurt. But if she asked Mamá, she was sure Mamá would disapprove. Mamá's own beautiful black hair reached all the way down to her waist, and she wore it pinned up in a bun at the nape of her neck. Once when Cecilia was younger, she had risen in the night to get a drink of water from the kitchen and had seen Papá brushing Mamá's long silky hair as she sat at her dressing table. She had never forgotten the lovely picture they made.

"I told you, I'll think about it," Cecilia told Belle. To herself, she worried that Mamá in her delicate state might react angrily to Cecilia cutting her hair without permission. They parted ways, and Belle sauntered over to her family's mercantile store while Cecilia walked the long porch to the kitchen door of her own home. As usual, the kitchen smelled of Mamá's good cooking. Today was Friday, baking day. The tantalizing aroma of freshly-baked bread filled Cecilia's nostrils and made her realize how hungry she was.

"*Ten, mi hija.* Here's a warm *mollete* for you," Mamá said as she slit open the anise-flavored bun and smeared it with lard. Cecilia ate it hungrily.

"I'm going to begin preparing the *chicos*," Cecilia said.

"Papá already made a fire in the *horno*, and Belia is waiting there to help you," her mother said.

Cecilia went to her room to change into her work dress. She placed the navy blue dress she had worn all week in a basket of dirty clothes. Next week she would wear the gray dress with the pink collar and pink belt. She took off Tía Sara's nice shoes and put on Elías's boots. Then she went back into the kitchen.

"Here's a surprise for you!" Tía Sara said. She held out a large package.

"My shoes! *¡Mis zapatos!*" Cecilia cried. "*Al fin llegaron, ¡qué bueno!* They finally came!" she said as she tore off the brown wrapping paper. She took the black pumps out and crossed her fingers, hoping the shoes would fit. Mamá had traced Cecilia's bare feet on a scrap of brown paper and mailed it in with the order. Cecilia slipped her feet into the shoes. They fit perfectly!

"Tía, thank you for letting me wear your shoes this week. *Te quiero mucho.* I love you so much," Cecilia said as she hugged her aunt.

"Dios tarda pero nunca olvida," Tía Sara said. "God takes his time, but he never forgets."

Cecilia ran to the back of the house where Papá had built an adobe *horno*, a beehive-shaped oven with an opening on one side. The *horno* was used for baking bread, smoking meat, or roasting corn. Papá had burned a fire in the *horno* all day and had cleared out the ashes. Now Cecilia and her younger sister Belia began to toss into the hot *horno* all the ears of corn Fito and Roberto had picked that morning, husk and all. Once they had finished, they sealed the opening with a metal plate and left the corn to roast overnight in the hot oven.

"Papá said we're going to have a *matanza* next month," Belia said anxiously. The slaughtering of a pig always upset her. "You don't think he's going to kill Lola, do you?" Belia had bottle-fed Lola from a piglet, and now Lola followed her all over the farmyard. Belia loved the fat pink pig as dearly as she loved all the other animals on the farm. It broke her heart every time Mamá killed a chicken or a guinea hen for Sunday lunch, or when Papá and Tío Santiago, Mamá's brother, killed a pig.

"No, Belia. I'm sure he's not going to choose Lola. He needs her to breed more pigs. Don't worry. He'll be slaughtering one of the old males," Cecilia said, trying to ease her sister's fear. But she herself didn't like the *matanza* any better than Belia. It wasn't a pleasant sight and most of the time, she couldn't even eat the meat for days afterwards. But Tía Sara always reminded them that the animals had been treated kindly and that the family had to eat.

"Ayúdame con la cena," Cecilia said. "Help me cook supper for Mamá. She's tired from baking bread today. And the boys will be coming in hungry from their chores."

The two sisters walked arm in arm to the kitchen. They would heat up a pot of beans and make a *sopa* of rice while their brothers finished feeding the livestock, cleaning out the chicken coops, and milking the cows. Everyone had work to do on the farm or in the house except Sylvia because she was the baby. The baby! Cecilia wondered what the new baby would be—a boy or a girl? Tía Sara was already mending hand-me-down baby clothes and hemming diapers made from flour sacks and old bedsheets. Cecilia could hear the gentle clacking of the sewing machine as Tía Sara pumped the foot pedal late into the night while Cecilia did her homework.

Cecilia hoped she could finish cleaning the kitchen quickly after supper so she would have time to begin reading the book she had checked out of the school library today—*The Story of My Life* by Helen Keller. Cecilia's favorite pastime was reading, and she read anything she could get her hands on. As there was no money in the house for books or magazines, Cecilia meant to make good use of the high school library. She could hardly wait to start reading the story of a girl who couldn't see or hear and yet lived a life filled with amazing accomplishments. Cecilia's teacher last year, Miss Malone, had recommended the auto-biography to Cecilia before she left for a new position in Silver City.

Mamá didn't approve of Cecilia spending so much time reading. Many times the *sopa* had burned or a pot had boiled over because Cecilia was engrossed in a book and forgot to check the stove. In fact, last year Fito had fallen into burning embers while Cecilia was supposed to be watching her young brothers as they played. Poor Fito had spent two months in bed with his foot elevated. Although Mamá hadn't said anything, Cecilia had blamed herself for the accident. Now there would be another baby to keep an eye on. Another demand on her precious time.

Why did I have to be the oldest girl in the family? she thought, and then instantly regretted it. She really did love her brothers and sisters and enjoyed taking care of them. It was just so hard to find time to do her homework and read her beloved books. Many nights she fell asleep at the kitchen table after supper while she studied or read by the light of a kerosene lamp. Then she would wake up at midnight, or later, and have to wash and put away all the dishes before she could go to bed. Whenever Mamá caught her asleep this way, she would become very angry and scold her.

"*Ay, Cecilia. Otra vez con tus libros.* There you are again wasting time with your books. You need to go to sleep like the rest of the family so you won't be so tired in the morning. *Ándale, vete a tu cuarto.* Go to your room. You can wash up in the morning."

But Cecilia would get up from the table, and no matter how late it was, would heat a tub of water and begin scrubbing the dried-on food from the dishes. Washing the dishes in the evening was *her* responsibility. Belia had other chores, and Mamá and Tía Sara had enough to do with the cooking, mending, canning, cleaning, and the multitude of other chores necessary in the farmhouse.

"Mira que buenas cocineras son mis hijas," Papá said as he entered the kitchen. As usual he wore overalls, a red bandana around his neck, and a straw hat to shield his face from the sun. "My good little cooks, what have you prepared for us today?" he teased his daughters. Cecilia laughed.

"Frijoles y sopita like every night," she said. "But since this is Friday, we have Mamá's fresh bread to eat with the beans and rice." Papá took a deep breath of the delicious aroma in the kitchen. Friday supper was everyone's favorite because no one in the valley baked bread as good as their mother's crusty loaves and little round buns, or *molletes.*

Papá washed his hands in the pan of soapy water by the stove and sat down at the table. Sylvia promptly jumped into his lap and curled there like a kitten. Cecilia poured him a cup of hot, fresh coffee that had been perking on the stove. Papá drank coffee at every meal from his special heavy white mug. As he drank, he made exaggerated slurping sounds that made Sylvia laugh.

Soon the entire family was seated around the table enjoying thick slices of fresh warm bread slathered with homemade butter. Cecilia jumped up every now and then to refill the coffee cups of her parents and her aunt. This was one of her responsibilities as the oldest daughter. The children all drank milk from the family's cows. One of Fito's jobs was to milk the cows every morning and every evening and carry the pails of milk carefully from the barn to the house. There was always fresh milk at breakfast and at supper. Sometimes Papá would milk the cows while the children stood in a row in front of him, and he would squirt a stream of milk at each of them, trying to aim it into their mouths. He would even squirt milk at the dogs and the barn cats. The children laughed at his antics and tried to position their heads to catch the stream of milk in their mouths. But Belia's gray cat Paloma would walk away indignantly to lick herself clean in a corner of the barn.

After supper Cecilia and Belia cleaned the kitchen while everyone sat outside on the front porch to enjoy the cool night air.

"I'm glad you're old enough to help me with the dishes," Cecilia said to Belia. "Now we can finish in half the time." The girls dried the last of the pans and put them away on the shelf. Then they too went out to sit on the porch and join the family in the idle conversation of the evening. Mamá and Papá sat in their rocking chairs. Sylvia sat in Tía Sara's lap, half asleep. She was a sweet, good-natured little girl who would no longer be the baby once the new one was born. Elías sat strumming his guitar while Fito and Roberto played a little game of their own invention on the porch steps. Cecilia and Belia sang the words to the melody softly as Elías strummed. A small fire burned in a bucket of manure, producing smoke that kept mosquitoes away.

Suddenly a figure appeared out of the darkness. *"Buenas noches. ¿Cómo están todos?"* It was Tío Santiago, Mamá's and Tía Sara's brother and the children's favorite uncle. He had walked over from his neighboring farm where he farmed and raised goats. Tío Santiago sat down to visit with his sister and her family. Pursing his lips together, he spit on the porch floor.

"Roberto, if you can run to Tío Ben's store and buy me a bag of tobacco before the spit dries, I'll give you a nickel. *¡Pronto, pronto, antes de que se seque la saliva!"* he told his nephew.

Roberto was off like a flash! A whole nickel! Just think of all the candy that would buy! He ran as fast as his legs could carry him and returned huffing and puffing with the little bag of tobacco clutched in his hand.

"Here you are, Tío. Is the spit dry?" he asked anxiously. Tío Santiago poked at the foamy spit with his toe.

"No se secó. It isn't dry. Here is your nickel," Tío Santiago said, chuckling. Roberto was his favorite among his nieces and nephews. Maybe it was because Roberto was the most mischievous one and always getting into trouble.

"Gracias, Tío. Mamá, can I go back to the store and buy some candy?" Roberto asked.

"Ay, Roberto, you'll just bother your Tío Ben. You know the store is closed right now," Mamá said.

"Por favor, Mamá. Please!" begged Roberto. All the other children began to clamor for her permission, and even Tía Sara said, *"Me gustaría algo dulce.* I would like a little something sweet."

Mamá nodded and Roberto was off again. He came back with a handful of grape-flavored suckers, Mamá's favorite candy.

"¡Ay, qué muchachito!" Mamá said. But she was touched that he had remembered what she liked.

For a while no one spoke as they savored the sweet candy. The only sound was the creaking of the rocking chairs and the chirping of the crickets in the garden in front of the porch. A light breeze ruffled the honeysuckle vines that twisted around the porch columns. Then Elías began to play a favorite song, *"Adelita."* Everyone joined in the singing:

> *"Si Adelita se fuera con otro,*
> *La seguiría por tierra y por mar.*
> *Si por mar en un buque de guerra,*
> *Y si por tierra en un tren militar.*
>
> *"Y si acaso me muero en la guerra*
> *Y en la tierra me he de quedar,*
> *Adelita por Dios te lo ruego,*
> *Que por mí no vayas a llorar."*

"If Adelita ran off with another,
I would follow her by land and by sea.
If by sea in a warship,
And if by land in a military train.

"And if I should die in battle
And my body is left in the ground,
Adelita, in God's name I beg you,
Not to cry for me."

As the evening got darker and darker, they could see nothing but the glow of the smoldering contents of the bucket and the tiny orange lights of Tío Santiago's and Papá's cigarettes. This was Cecilia's favorite time of day—all work done, everyone sitting together, laughing and singing. Soon Tío Santiago would amble home in the dark, and they would all go in to bed. Cecilia would begin her homework, reading well into the night. Later, slipping exhausted into bed, she would think of Johnny, hope that tomorrow would be the day a letter arrived from him, and then cry herself to sleep as she did every night. But right now, at this moment, everything was perfect, everything was just as it should be. She leaned her head against Mamá's knees and looked up at the sky. It seemed as if all the stars were twinkling just for her.

CECILIA WAS UP early Saturday morning. She splashed cold water on her face from a basin on the dresser in the bedroom she shared with Belia. Then, smiling mischievously, she sprinkled cold water on Belia as she slept.

"Levántate, dormilona. Wake up, sleepyhead. We have to take the corn out of the *horno.* We can have roasted corn for breakfast!" she told Belia.

The girls dressed hurriedly and ran outside. Papá was already pulling away the iron plate which blocked the hole in the beehive oven. A blast of steam poured out, and the wonderful smell of fresh roasted corn filled the air.

"Ándale, muchachas. Help me fill the tubs with corn. Belia, take these to the kitchen for breakfast," Papá ordered. He had been up since before daylight, feeding the horses, pigs, cows, and chickens. The boys were already milking the cows, pumping water, and chopping wood.

That morning, along with the usual oatmeal, beans, and chile, the family feasted on roasted *elotes,* corn on the cob dripping with homemade butter. This would be the last of the fresh corn from the summer harvest. But they would still get to eat corn all winter in the form of *chicos,* dried corn cooked in red chile sauce.

After breakfast, Cecilia and Belia spent the rest of the morning hanging the roasted ears of corn on wires strung inside the *dispensa,* the large storage shed next to the house. They hung corn from every available hook and nail on the walls and on hooks dangling from the ceiling until all the ears were hung to dry. Once the corn dried in the husks, it would be taken down and stored in burlap bags. To prepare *chicos*, the boys would put the dry ears of corn through a grinder while they turned the handle. The kernels would pop off into a pan. Mamá would soak the kernels overnight in water until they softened. Then she would boil them in seasoned red chile. Mamá's *chicos* were delicious and one of the children's favorite foods, especially during Lent when they couldn't eat meat.

That afternoon, when Cecilia had finally finished all her chores, she sat under the old, enormous cottonwood tree where she loved to read. Today she was reading Helen Keller's autobiography. She especially loved the part where the young Helen had learned to spell with sign language when Anne Sullivan placed her hands under the water flowing from a pump. It reminded Cecilia of her own daily chore of pumping water. But even Helen Keller's enthralling story couldn't keep Cecilia from brooding over Johnny. Surely a letter would come soon. He had promised! She closed her eyes and tried to picture him as he had looked the last time she had seen him. He and Elías had looked so handsome galloping across the fields on their horses.

Suddenly, a loud rattling noise interrupted her reverie. She looked up to see a most curious sight. She had never seen anything like it. A motor vehicle, some sort of car and truck combination with valises and boxes tied to the roof and to its sides, jerked noisily down the road. It seemed to be overflowing with people. Arms and legs stuck out of windows, and blonde heads bobbed up and down as the car stopped and started, dark smoke belching from the exhaust pipe. The strange vehicle gave a violent lurch forward and then with a loud bang, amid a cloud of thick black smoke, came to a sudden and abrupt stop in front of Cecilia's house.

CHAPTER 3

No juzgues el hombre por su vestido;
Dios hizo el uno, el sastre el otro.

> Do not judge a man by his clothing;
> God made one, the tailor the other.

Cecilia jumped up from under the tree where she was sitting. Her book fell to the ground. She stood rooted in surprise and awe. As she watched wide-eyed, bodies seemed to spill out of the strange-looking car, one blonde child after another. And then as if things couldn't get any stranger, an enormously fat woman with long white hair was helped out of the car by a tall skinny man in worn overalls. A thin woman holding a baby in her arms was the last one to step out of the car. Cecilia's eyes grew wider. The thin woman's head was framed with the reddest, frizziest hair Cecilia had ever seen. Her hair floated in the afternoon breeze making her head look as if it was on fire. The towheaded children ran up and down the road followed by a small yapping brown dog.

"Water! I need water!" the old lady cried as she fanned herself with a bit of cardboard. The man helped her lean against the car as the woman holding the baby looked on helplessly. Amidst all the confusion and the shouting by the children, Cecilia noticed a young girl about her own age standing quietly and looking back at Cecilia with pale blue eyes. She was wearing the shabbiest, most faded dress Cecilia had ever seen on anyone. As if reading Cecilia's thoughts, the young girl crossed her arms across her chest and turned sideways to hide her face.

"I'll get water!" Cecilia said and then ran as fast as she could to the house.

"*¡Mamá, Mamá, venga, venga!*" she cried. "Come see the people outside! They need water!"

Mamá came into the kitchen, irritated that she had been disturbed from her nap. Due to her pregnancy, she needed to rest in the afternoons before cooking supper.

"*¿Qué dices, niña? ¿Qué pasa?*" she asked. "Why are you calling me?"

"Mamá, there are some strange people outside. I think the lady is sick. She needs water. Mamá, come look! Who can they be?" Cecilia asked.

Mamá rolled down her sleeves to make herself more presentable and then walked out onto the porch. By now all the children had settled down, and the entire family was standing in front of their useless car along with the little brown dog, which mercifully had ceased its barking. With the exception of the old woman, they were thin and gaunt-looking, and Cecilia noticed all of them were as shabbily dressed as the young girl. The tall man took off his cap and stepped forward.

"Ma'am, would you be so kind as to give us some water. My ma ain't feeling too good. We've come a long way today, and she cain't take all the bumps in the road like the young folks. Please, ma'am." He stood nervously twisting his cap in his hands.

Mamá could understand English better than she could speak it. She turned to Cecilia and said, "*Diles que pasen. Les daremos agua y comida.* We will give them water and food." She nodded at the forlorn group and went inside to start heating up beans and whatever else she could find in the *dispensa* to offer them. Even though she complained about Papá giving things away and giving haircuts for free, she too had a tender side and hated to see any living creature go hungry. Tramps passing through seemed to know to stop at her door for a hot meal. Many times Cecilia came home from school to find a hobo sitting at the kitchen table eating beans and tortillas while Mamá sat eyeing him at the other end of the table, a sharp kitchen knife hidden under her apron.

"My mother says to come in. She'll give you food and water," Cecilia told them.

The three young boys ran to the kitchen door. Behind them followed their father supporting his old mother, his wife holding their baby daughter, and the young blonde girl who had stared so intently at Cecilia. The girl stopped in front of Cecilia.

"Hi, I'm Jeannie," she told Cecilia shyly.

"I'm Cecilia. Where are you from?" she asked.

"We've come all the way from Oklahoma," Jeannie answered. "We're on our way to California. My pa is going to get a job with my uncle in Los Angeles. He's good at fixing automobiles. Good thing, too, or we couldn't have made it this far in that old thing," she said, tossing her head in the direction of the broken-down vehicle.

"Oklahoma!" said Cecilia. "That's really far from here. What is it like in Oklahoma?"

"Oh, it's bad right now. Real bad. We ain't had no rain at all. Ain't nothin' but dirt and dust. We're going to California where it's green, and my uncle says there's plenty of water there. Says he can get my pa a job working on automobiles, so we'll be all right," Jeannie said. Cecilia pretended not to see the tears starting up in Jeannie's blue eyes.

"Come inside. My mother would like your family to eat with us," Cecilia said as she led her new friend into the kitchen. Already the tantalizing aroma of fried bacon filled the air as Mamá prepared a feast of bacon, beans, fried potatoes, and *molletes*.

"Jeep, you stay outside," Jeannie ordered the little brown dog.

"I'll fix a bowl of scraps for Jeep," said Cecilia. "Oh, look! He's playing with Chata. That's my sister Belia's dog. We call her Chata because she has a pug nose." The two frisky little dogs romped on the porch while Paloma, Belia's gray cat, looked down with disdain from her perch on the wooden gate.

The family from Oklahoma sat at the table and ate as if they hadn't had a meal in days. The young boys had rough manners, but their exhausted, frail mother seemed too pre-occupied with the baby to notice. Jeannie sat quietly and ate daintily, although she was as hungry as everyone else.

"Lord a mercy, that was good!" said the old lady with the enormous stomach and the long white hair. She sat back in her chair and closed her eyes.

"We thank you kindly for your hospitality," said the father. "Could we impose a little longer and ask if we may spend the night outside your house? My ma and my poor wife are exhausted. We won't be no trouble at all. These young-uns will behave themselves, don't you worry."

Just then Papá and the boys came into the kitchen for their supper. They stood completely surprised to see anoth-er family sitting at the table eating their supper.

"Come inside, we're eating supper," said Tía Sara to Elías, Fito, and Roberto. She had been helping Mamá with the meal.

"*¿Qué es esto?*" Papá asked. "Hey Bob, hey Bob," he said to the man. Papá called all Anglo men "Bob."

Cecilia explained how the family was traveling from Oklahoma and had broken down in front of the house. She told Papá they would like to spend the night on their property.

"*Claro que sí. Mi casa es su casa.* Welcome, welcome," he told the father, whose name turned out to be Ollie Vetter. "*Que se queden en la casita de atrás,*" Papá told Cecilia.

Cecilia explained to Mr. Vetter that they could stay in the *jacal*—the adobe shed behind the house. The little building wasn't much, but at least they would have a roof over their heads. She felt a warm glow inside when she saw the Vetter children's faces light up and Mrs. Vetter breathe a deep sigh of relief when they heard Papá's offer. All of them seemed much happier and more relaxed after the hearty meal. Cecilia thought of one of Tía Sara's sayings, *"Panza llena, corazón contento."* It *was* true that things look better on a full stomach. Suddenly she realized how lucky her family was to have this wonderful old home to live in, their own land to grow crops, and plenty of food on the table. This poor family had nothing except their car and the few household items they had been able to fit into it when they left their home.

Elías led the family to the shed behind the house. Mrs. Vetter ordered her boys to untie all the suitcases from the car and carry them inside. Fito showed them where the water pump and the outhouse were. Mamá sent over a basket of eggs, some salt pork, and *molletes* for their breakfast. Mrs. Vetter would have to cook over an outdoor fire, but she was used to it as the family had been camping out and living on canned beans since they left Oklahoma. Tía Sara took the Vetter baby into the house to give her a bath, giving Mrs. Vetter a chance to rest.

While all this was happening, Papá and Mr. Vetter were having a discussion while Elías helped translate. The Vetter car had broken down in front of the house, and Mr. Vetter had no money to pay for repairs. Papá told him that he could find a job a few miles up the road where a new dam was being built. The company building Caballo Dam was always in need of workers. Mr. Vetter would pay Papá a small amount of rent, and the Vetter children could help out on the farm. Papá was still picking cotton and would soon be making cane syrup, and he could use the extra help. As soon as Mr. Vetter earned enough money to repair the car, they would be on their way to California. The two men shook hands and called it a deal.

The next day, after *misa,* Mamá sent her children over to the shed to show the Vetters how to make it more habitable. Elías and the boys brought in buckets of damp dirt and threw it on the floor. Then all the children walked around the small room, stamping the floor with their feet, packing down the earth. As they marched in a circle, Belia led them in a chant:

> *"Pin, pin jarabín*
> *La tuerta clueca pasó por aquí*
> *Convidando a sus hijos*
> *Y menos a mí.*
> *Cuchara, salero*
> *Esconde tu dedo*
> *En la lomita de San Miguel."*

"Pin, pin jarabín
The one-eyed hen passed by here
Gathering up her children
But not me.
Spoon, saltshaker
Hide your finger
In the little hill of San Miguel."

The Vetter boys had never heard a word of Spanish in their lives, but they were lively and bright and soon had memorized the chant, part of a children's finger game. However, Andy, Leroy, and Barnett Vetter could not roll their *r*'s with their tongues, and Fito and Roberto fell on the dirt floor with laughter at the boys' pronunciation of the Spanish words.

Once the fresh dirt had been packed down, Mr. Vetter and Elías hung a large piece of unbleached muslin across the ceiling. This was called a *manta del cielo*. The "blanket of the sky" nailed from wall to wall kept straw, dirt, rain, and insects from falling into the room from the straw and wooden *vigas*, or beams, that made up the roof. Then they brought in an old wooden table for the family to eat on and a few wooden benches from the barn. Grandma Vetter rested her enormous frame on an old rocker outside the *jacal*, basking in the afternoon sun, while Mrs. Vetter perked a pot of coffee on an outdoor fire. As Mrs. Vetter bent over the pot, her wild red hair lifted in the breeze, as if competing with the dancing orange flames of the fire.

"Do you like to read?" Cecilia asked Jeannie as they sat together talking under Cecilia's favorite cottonwood tree.

"I don't read too good," Jeannie answered. "But I love to look at the pictures."

"I can help you learn to read better, if you want," Cecilia said. "Are you going to go to school while you're here? My old school is just down the road."

"Pa says we won't be here that long. He says the boys have to stay here and work for your pa to pay the rent. He says we can go to school in California," Jeannie answered wistfully. "But I'd like to learn to read better."

"Well, I'll lend you my books while you are here so you can practice reading. I'll bring home some books from my school library with lots of pictures, too," Cecilia promised. "Look at this one." She held out the autobiography of Helen Keller that she was reading. Jeannie took it and started to read the first paragraph aloud. She read slowly and with great difficulty—even the little words were hard for her to recognize. Cecilia tried to hide her surprise as she helped Jeannie pronounce the words. What kind of life had this poor girl led that she couldn't even read and yet was almost as old as Cecilia? Cecilia thought about all the wonderful books she had read, all the exciting places she had visited through her books, all the fascinating things she had learned, and she realized that Jeannie had missed out on all of this. She felt so lucky that she had been allowed to go to elementary school where Miss Malone had taught her to love reading. And how lucky, too, that Mamá was letting her go to high school where there was a wonderful library filled with books. She felt proud that Papá was helping this poor family. She would try to help Jeannie learn to read better, even if it was only for a few weeks.

AT SCHOOL, Cecilia had made another new friend. Her name was Loretta Peacock and her father owned Peacock's Clothing Store in Hatch. Cecilia and Loretta sat next to each other in algebra and in home economics. Loretta reminded Cecilia of Jeannie. She had pale blonde hair, the color of dried hay, and light blue eyes. Like Jeannie, she was pretty, soft-spoken, and shy. She was also a very poor student who could read only slightly better than Jeannie and had no math skills whatsoever. In fact, she had failed the first two algebra exams.

"My father is going to kill me if I flunk algebra," she wailed to Cecilia. "He was such a good student when he was young, he thinks I should be, too. I try and try, but I just can't understand all those numbers. I'm just stupid, that's all. What am I going to do?"

"Of course, you are not stupid!" Cecilia said. "Can't your mother help you?" Cecilia asked. She knew Loretta's parents were both educated and wealthy, unlike her own. They owned the most expensive clothing store in town and lived in a beautiful brick house. Mrs. Peacock even drove her own car! Cecilia had often envied Loretta's beautiful dresses—a different one every day, and she wondered what it must be like to go home to such a beautiful house. Loretta's life seemed so grand and easy. Someday Cecilia would live in a beautiful brick house and drive her own car, too!

"My mother doesn't care what I do," Loretta said with a trace of bitterness in her voice. "She's too busy playing cards every day with her friends or going to meetings and things like that. And my father is always busy in the store. Anyway, he thinks I should do it on my own the way he did."

Cecilia couldn't even imagine a mother who played cards every day and went to meetings. Her own mother spent every day cooking, washing, scrubbing, ironing, canning, taking care of the children—the household chores were endless. Poor Mamá now had another baby coming, along with a lot more work! Cecilia thought about all the work Mamá did for her family, and a great feeling of love welled up in her chest. Poor Loretta! Imagine having a mother who didn't care what you did! Cecilia wouldn't trade places with her for anything.

"I can help you with algebra. I love math. It's easy, you'll see. But we'll have to study during lunch because I can't stay after school. I have to ride the bus home," Cecilia said.

"Oh, Cecilia, you're so smart! Why, you're the smartest girl I know. Will you really help me? Can you come to my house on Saturday?" Loretta asked.

"Oh, no! I have to help my mother in the house. She depends on me," Cecilia said proudly. "Besides, my mother would never let me go into town alone."

"Could I come to *your* house Saturday afternoon?"

Loretta asked. "Please? I don't know what else to do, and we have another test soon," she pleaded.

Cecilia thought of her sprawling old adobe home surrounded by sheds and animal pens. She thought about the *jacal* behind the house where the wild Oklahoma boys played their rough games, and the fat, toothless old woman sat sunning herself at the door. She thought about Mamá and Tía Sara cooking in the kitchen, their faces sweaty and red from the hot stove. She thought about Mamá speaking only Spanish and not understanding what Loretta would say. She thought about Loretta's grand house and elegant mother who always wore a strand of pearls around her neck when she came to pick up Loretta after school in her shiny blue car. Cecilia hesitated.

"All right. I should be finished with all my chores after lunch. That's when I usually get time to read. I guess I can help you with algebra then," Cecilia said hesitantly.

"Oh, thank you! I'll get Albert Castle to drive me over. You know him—he's the cute boy who sits behind you in science class," Loretta said.

Cecilia's mouth went dry. Oh, no! What would Loretta and Albert think of her home and her family? She had just started to get over her embarrassment from wearing Elías' boots the first week of school. Why did they have to come to her house? Their homes in town were so different from hers. And what would Mamá think of a girl who rode alone in a car with a boy? Would Mamá embarrass her by not allowing Loretta and Albert in the house?

As Loretta smiled at Cecilia, her eyes were filled with tears of gratitude. Loretta may have been pretty and wealthy, but she had always been made to feel incompetent and slow by her parents. She was desperate to pass the upcoming algebra exam. Cecilia felt sorry for her friend. She herself had always excelled in all her classes. Math came so easily to her. She would tutor Loretta the same way she tutored Elías last spring when he took the high school entrance exam.

"I'll see you Saturday, then," Loretta said as she walked toward the big blue car waiting to take her home.

On Saturday Cecilia finished all her chores early with Jeannie's help. By the time Loretta and Albert drove up, the two girls were waiting for them on the porch where Elías had joined them. Fito, Roberto, and the Vetter boys were playing cops and robbers in the garden in front of the house. Tía Sara, looking serene and beautiful, sat on the porch with Sylvia in her lap.

"Would you like to ride horses?" Elías asked Albert. They were both on the school football team. Albert was a cheerful, easygoing young man, and he and Elías had become friends.

"Swell!" Albert said. The two boys ran off to ride horses while the girls studied.

"Come inside the *sala*," Cecilia said. "I mean, the parlor."

"How pretty!" Loretta exclaimed as she looked about her. Mamá's *sala* was used only on special occasions. All her best furniture was there along with a beautiful piano that had come all the way from St. Louis, Missouri. Crocheted doilies, made by Tía Sara, covered the arms of the sofa. A beautiful lace tablecloth lay on the round table in the center of the room. The three girls gathered around the table and spread open their books. Cecilia began to explain one problem after another to Loretta as Jeannie looked on. Soon they were laughing and joking and even talking about Albert and the other boys at school.

Mamá came in with a tray of hot chocolate and apricot *empanadas*. She had made the little turnovers using apricots from their own orchard that she had put up in jars in the summer. She smiled at the girls and left without speaking. The *empanadas* were delicious, and the girls ate them hungrily.

"Your mother is beautiful!" Loretta exclaimed. "Her hair is fabulous. No wonder you have such thick shiny hair. I've been so jealous of you!"

Cecilia was shocked. *She* had been jealous of Loretta's soft blonde curls which were cut short in the latest style. Even Jeannie wore her hair bobbed to the chin with curly bangs.

"You should cut your hair like your cousin Belle's," Loretta said. "You have those beautiful brown eyes. I think short curls around your face would really bring them out."

"Well, I *have* been thinking about it," Cecilia admitted. She was still worried about what Mamá would say if she wanted to cut her hair. Most of the other farm girls had cut their hair short like the town girls. Still, she had worn her hair in long braids all her life. Could she really cut them off?

"You've helped me a lot with these problems. I think I

understand how to do them. Thank you so much! And thank you for inviting me to your beautiful house. Everything is so pretty and lively here. Your family is so nice. I wish I had brothers and sisters. I'm an only child, so I'm alone most of the time," she said wistfully as she looked at all the family photographs in their oval frames on the parlor walls. "And your brother Elías is so handsome!" she added with a gleam in her eye. The three girls giggled.

After Albert and Loretta drove off, Cecilia went into the kitchen and gave Mamá a hug.

"*¿Qué te pasa, hija?*" Mamá asked. "What is wrong?"

"*Nada.* Nothing. I just can't wait for the baby to be born," Cecilia said. How could she explain to Mamá how foolish and ashamed she felt at being nervous about Loretta's visit. She wanted Mamá to know somehow that she was proud of her and Papá and all the rest of the family.

Later as Cecilia lay in bed waiting for sleep, she thought about Loretta and Jeannie, her two new friends. Loretta's family had so much money! Yet she seemed so unhappy, so lonely, so insecure! Jeannie was poorer than anyone Cecilia knew—poor in money and poor in learning. Why, she could barely read! Cecilia was beginning to understand that there were many different types of poverty. Compared to Loretta's family and Jeannie's lack of education, Cecilia was rich. She thought for a moment about that. Why, she *was* rich! It didn't matter if you lived in a mansion, a farmhouse, or a *jacal* as long as you were part of a loving, happy family. Now Cecilia understood what Tía Sara meant when she said, *"Más vale poco y bueno que mucho y malo."* Cecilia knew Mamá and Papá loved her and wanted only the best for her. And she had her books which she loved second only to her family. At that moment, Cecilia felt very rich indeed!

CECILIA LOVED fall more than any other season. The air was always filled with wonderful smells—mesquite wood burning in the kitchen stove and chile roasting over an open flame outside. Even the fallen leaves, rotting in the earth, had a rich, musty smell. But the smell Cecilia loved best was the sweet odor of cane juice boiling in a pan over a hot fire until it turned into molasses. The making of molasses, or *miel de caña,* was a once-a-year event that all the children looked forward to. But it was hard work, and Papá was glad to have the Vetter boys to help this year.

"*Ándale, muchachos. A trabajar,"* he told them. "Let's get to work." Papá, with the help of Elías, Roberto, and Fito, had already cut down the *caña* and piled the stalks in the barn. Now he put Andy, Leroy, and Barnett to work stripping the foliage off the stalks and cutting the long stalks into shorter pieces. Then the boys fed the stalks by hand into the *trapiche,* the grinding mill that ground the stalks and extracted the juice. The *trapiche* had a long stick on one side to which their horse Valiente was tied. As the horse walked round and round, the mill wheels turned and ground the cane. The cane juice ran into a wooden vat on the side of the mill as the stalks of cane were crushed. Then Papá poured the cane juice into a *paila,* a huge rectangular metal pan made especially for boiling the juice. The pan was about 5 feet long, 4 feet wide, and 2 feet deep. Fito and Roberto used to make Mamá angry by using the pan as a raft in the irrigation canal in the summer.

Papá placed the pan on adobe bricks and built a roaring fire underneath. The boys fed wood to the fire under the pan, and the juice boiled and boiled for hours. Papá liked to cook it at night when the air was cool. All night he stood over the pan of boiling juice, stirring and stirring with a long wooden paddle. The tired, sleepy boys went to bed, but Papá and Elías stayed up adding more wood to the fire and watching over the liquid until it turned into syrup.

In the morning Papá came into the house yelling *"¡Ya está la miel! ¡Arriba con los velices!* Lift up your suitcases! Get up! Get up! The molasses is ready!" All the children, still in their pajamas, ran out with bowls to sample the sweet syrup. And in the kitchen, Mamá was busy making hot biscuits for a special breakfast of biscuits and molasses.

Later Papá poured the syrup into *barriles*, large wooden barrels which were stored in the *dispensa,* which also held barrels of apples, burlap bags of dried chile, and jars of canned fruits and vegetables that Mamá and Cecilia had put up all summer. They would use the rich dark syrup to sweeten oatmeal and cookies, and to pour over hotcakes. There would be plenty to eat this winter, *gracias a Dios.*

One of the children's favorite sweet treats was sugared watermelon rind. Papá grew a watermelon called *chilicayote*. It was yellow inside instead of red and tasted a little salty. The family would eat the melon, and then Mamá would peel and cut the rind into squares which she put into a barrel of cane syrup. In a few weeks the pieces of melon rind would be candied and delicious! Mamá let the children take turns deciding what to have for dessert after supper from the stores in the *dispensa*. Roberto always chose the candied watermelon rind. Mamá would make him roll up his sleeve and scrub his right arm so he could stick his arm deep into the barrel and fish out the pieces of rind. Cecilia never liked to stick her arm into the barrel because afterwards, no matter how hard she washed her arm, she still felt sticky. But she loved eating the sweet, sugary squares.

THE VETTER BOYS and Cecilia's brothers had become great friends. After all their chores were done, they ran wild over the fields playing cowboys and Indians, building forts, shooting pecans off the trees with their slingshots, and scattering the chickens with their yells and laughter. They pestered Cecilia and Jeannie when they were reading or sharing secrets and annoyed Mamá and Tía Sara in the kitchen. Mrs. Vetter didn't seem to know, or care, what her boys were doing. She was a slightly-built woman who never said much and always seemed to have the baby in her arms. Her fat mother-in-law didn't help at all to keep the *jacal* clean or to cook for the family on the outside fire. She just sat in the old rocker in the sun on warm days or lay on a cot inside when it was cool. Mr. Vetter was off working at the dam, so the boys were free to do as they pleased once Papá didn't need them.

"Vayan a limpiar el gallinero," Mamá ordered one afternoon when they angered her by trampling some of the plants in her garden. "Go clean out the chicken coop. And bring me any eggs you find."

As the boys raked the chicken droppings from the hay on the floor of the chicken coop, Andy Vetter said, "Let's play a trick on Grammaw. You know how she'll eat anything. Let's see if she'll eat this." He pulled some crackers from his pocket and used a twig to spread the crackers with chicken droppings. He piled the gray-green muck on the crackers while the other boys doubled over with laughter. Together they marched to the *jacal* where the obese old woman sat sunning herself in her rocker.

"Hey, Grammaw, Mrs. Gonzales sent you a snack," Andy told his grandmother as he held out the crackers. The other boys, along with Belia who had been watching curiously, stood gritting their teeth trying not to laugh.

The old woman took a cracker and eyed it carefully. She put it up to her nose and sniffed. Then she said, "You rascals git away from here before I whup you good. How dumb do you think I am?" Then she turned her head toward the door and yelled, "Rowena, come see what your boys tried to feed me!"

The boys ran off and hid under the bridge over the irrigation ditch, laughing until their stomachs hurt. Belia was incensed. They had told the woman that her mother had sent the nasty crackers! The Vetters would think Mamá was crazy! Belia ran home to tell on the boys. Mamá was napping, but Tía Sara was in the kitchen.

"Tía, you should see what all the boys did! *Fueron muy malos.* They did a bad thing!" Belia said breathlessly. Tía Sara listened to the story with amusement. She knew her nephews were high-spirited and energetic and always getting into trouble. And the Vetter boys were even worse since they weren't in school and had no real supervision at home.

"Don't worry, *niña.* The old woman knows her grandsons and the tricks they play. She will know your mother didn't send her those crackers. Besides, they will learn a lesson some day. *Como dice el dicho, 'Si escupes para arriba, te va a caer en la cara.'* If you spit in the air, it will fall on your face," she said. "Sit down and drink some of the *atole* I just made." Belia drank the hot, sweet cornmeal gruel. It felt good in her stomach on this cool fall day. She forgot all about her anger and never told Mamá what the boys had done. Fito and Roberto were lucky, for Mamá would have whipped their behinds with the leather *chicote* if she had known.

Later that evening when everyone was outside trying to catch the last rays of the sun, the boys were sitting on Tío Ben's car. Tío Ben had stopped to visit on his way home and had parked his car under a large cottonwood tree.

Papá and Tío Ben were asking Mr. Vetter about his work at Caballo Dam.

"Tío, can I start your car, please?" asked Elías. He liked to sit in the car and pretend that he could drive. Although he loved riding his horse Panky, he would have given anything to have a car and know how to drive like some of the town boys. Tío Ben nodded, and Elías got into the driver's seat. Andy, Leroy, Barnett, Fito, and Roberto stood around the outside of the car. Elías turned the key in the ignition. The brake was set, so he stepped on the gas pedal and gunned the motor. A loud bang like a gunshot filled the air as the car backfired. The noise frightened a large flock of buzzards that had been roosting in the branches of the tree above the car. They flew off in fright flapping their wings, and as they flew their droppings rained down on the boys below. Everyone on the porch broke out laughing as they saw the poor boys get pelted with fresh, wet bird droppings! The slimy muck fell on their hair, on their faces, and all over their clothes.

"*¡Ay, mira lo que pasó!*" cried Fito. He tried to wipe his face with his sleeve and just succeeded in smearing the mess worse across his face.

"Pa, look what happened!" cried Andy as he ran to his father. The younger boys started to cry and rub their eyes with their dirty hands.

Mr. Vetter could hardly speak for laughing, but he managed to say, "Ain't you fellers glad them weren't cows up in that tree?"

CHAPTER 4

En la casa llena, pronto se cena.
In a full house, supper is soon ready.

Cecilia had found a confidante in Jeannie. The two girls had become good friends over the past few weeks. Jeannie even slept with Cecilia and Belia in their room since there was so little space in the *jacal*. While Cecilia was at school, Jeannie helped Mamá with household chores. In the evenings, Cecilia had extra time to help Jeannie improve her reading. Jeannie was trying to read *A Girl of the Limberlost*, Cecilia's favorite book that Mamá had given her last Christmas.

"It's such a romantic story," Jeannie sighed. "Elnora is so poor but she gets educated and falls in love. Do you love anyone, Cecilia?"

Cecilia blushed as she thought of Johnny, so far away in El Paso. She hadn't seen him in months. Where was the letter he had promised to write? She certainly couldn't write him first! What would he think? Besides, she didn't have his new address. She decided to tell Jeannie her secret.

"Yes, I like a boy. His name is Johnny and he gave me a valentine last year—and two kisses! I thought he liked me too, but he moved away and he hasn't even written me," she said, a sob catching in her throat. She thought of the old saying, *"Para olvidar un querer, tres meses de no ver."* She and Johnny hadn't seen each other for much more than three months, and that was exactly how long the old saying said it took to forget someone you love. She felt an icy fear deep in the pit of her stomach. Johnny must have forgotten all about her by now—out of sight, out of mind. "Oh, Jeannie! He probably has a girlfriend in El Paso!" Cecilia said, finally breaking down into tears.

"Oh, no! I'm sure he doesn't," Jeannie said as she tried to comfort her friend. She put her arm around Cecilia's shoulder. "Don't cry, Cecilia. I'm sure he still likes you. Boys don't like to write letters, that's all. He probably thinks about you all the time, you're so pretty and sweet. Maybe you could write him first?"

Cecilia was horrified at the idea. "I could never do that! I just couldn't. He would think I'm chasing him. Besides, my mother would be so angry if she found out."

"Well, I'll just bet one of these days you'll get a letter," Jeannie said. "I know *I'll* send you one when we get to California."

Cecilia hugged her friend. "And I'll write you back. I promise," Cecilia said. And true to their words, the two girls would write to each other for the rest of their lives.

At the moment, though, they were busy roasting the last bit of green chile that hadn't turned red yet. Usually Mamá oversaw this tedious task, but now her pregnancy was too advanced, and she spent every afternoon resting in bed. Jeannie washed the mud off the long green chiles and poked them with a fork. Then Cecilia laid them on a grill over a fire outside in the cool air. Chile was roasted indoors only when the weather was bad. The pungent smell of roasting chile was wonderful, but Mamá didn't like it all over the house. Cecilia and Jeannie carefully watched the chiles scorch and turned them over before they burned. When the chiles were blackened and blistered on all sides, they put them in a deep bowl and covered them with a flour sack to trap the steam. The steam caused the skins to loosen. When the chiles had cooled, Cecilia and Jeannie pulled off the skin and picked out the seeds using their bare hands. Afterwards, even though they soaked them in cool water, the girls' hands burned for hours from handling the hot peppers.

Cecilia carried the roasted, cleaned peppers into the house for Mamá to make *chile rellenos* for supper. She would also use the chiles to make a salsa with tomatoes and onions. Finally, she would chop up the chiles and boil them in milk to eat with fried potatoes. Jeannie and her family had gotten used to eating the spicy food that Mamá shared with them, and now Jeannie looked forward to eating the delicious *rellenos* stuffed with cheese, rolled in egg batter, and fried in lard. Tomorrow a *chile relleno burrito* would be in all the children's school lunches.

The smell of the roasted chile made the girls hungry. Inside the warm kitchen, Cecilia cut thick slices of bread and spread them with *cajeta de membrillo*, jelly made from quince fruit that grew on a tree in their orchard. Quince fruit looked like pears except that it was very sour and dry and only good for making jelly. The *cajeta de membrillo* was sticky and sweet, and the girls ate ravenously. Cecilia noticed that Jeannie's face had softened and filled out due to the heartier meals she was eating on the farm. In fact, all the Vetter family had put on weight—even Grammaw.

Mamá was not feeling good, so Cecilia had to start the dough for tomorrow's breadmaking. She mixed dried yeast, water, and flour until it formed a dough. Then she placed the lump of dough in a bowl and sat it on the warming shelf above the stove so that it could rise overnight. In the morning she would get up early and knead the dough again, leaving it to rise once more before Mamá made her bread.

"There is a dance at school Saturday night," Cecilia told Jeannie as they wiped flour off the table and swept the floor. "They call it a homecoming dance. Belle and Virginia are going. I want to go, but I don't think Mamá will let me."

"She might if your brother goes, won't she?" asked Jeannie. She would love to go to a dance, but she was too shy, and besides, she had nothing to wear but one other dress as old and faded as the one she was wearing.

Cecilia thought about Elías. He would be playing in the football game Friday afternoon, but she was afraid he wouldn't want to go to the dance on Saturday. Elías didn't like social activities. He wasn't interested in meeting girls. He was already in love with Isabel, a dark, pretty girl from Rincón. Isabel wouldn't be at the dance as she lived too far away.

"Let's go ask him," Jeannie suggested. The girls found Elías in the barn.

"No, I don't want to go to the dance," he said emphatically. "*Ya no me molestes. No quiero ir.* You know I don't like things like that. And don't bother me anymore about it."

Cecilia knew how shy and introverted Elías was. She also knew he was going to high school so that Mamá would allow her to go as well. He felt he had done enough for her already.

"Ask your mother tonight. You've done so much work today, maybe she'll say yes," Jeannie said.

"You don't know my mamá," Cecilia said.

After supper when the family was settling down for the night, Cecilia approached her mother hesitantly.

"*Mamá, quiero ir al baile.* I would like to go to the school dance Saturday night with Belle and Virginia."

Mamá looked at Cecilia sternly. "*¿Solas?*" she asked. "Alone?"

"A school bus will come this way to pick up anyone who

wants to go. We will all go together. The bus will bring us back," Cecilia explained. "Everyone is going."

"Is Elías going? No? Well, then you cannot go without your brother to watch over you. A proper young lady does not go out at night without her family. What would all your *tías* say? What would people think of me if I let you behave that way? Now do not pester me about it. I am not feeling good right now. I am going to my room to rest," Mamá said firmly, putting an end to the discussion.

Cecilia ran to her room, tears stinging her eyes. She threw herself on her bed. Although she tried not to, she broke out in sobs. Jeannie and Belia tried to comfort her.

"It's not fair! I never get to do anything because of Elías! He can do anything he wants, but I can't because I'm a girl!" Cecilia cried.

"I guess I won't get to do anything either when I'm older," said Belia. And she started to cry, too.

"Don't cry, Cecilia. We'll have fun here reading from our books," Jeannie said. But the other two girls looked so sad and tearful that Jeannie began to sniffle. Soon all three were sitting on the bed crying.

Cecilia thought of Belle, Virginia, Loretta, and all the other girls with more modern parents. They would be having fun at the dance while she stayed home. She would spend Saturday night heating pails of water and bathing the younger children in the big tin tub in the kitchen, while her friends were dancing and laughing together. And in a few months, she would be boiling baby diapers!

It's just not fair! I don't know why Mamá treats me like this. I'm suffocating here. I'm nothing but a farm girl. And Mamá cares more about what other people think than about my feelings. When I grow up, I'm going to do whatever I want! Cecilia thought. As she untied her braids and brushed her long hair before getting into bed, an idea formed in her head.

Belle is right. I do look old-fashioned in these braids, she thought. *All the other girls have short hair, and the girls in El Paso must look very modern and stylish. If Johnny were here, he would think I looked old-fashioned and like a little girl. I hate my braids now. I should be able to do whatever I want with my own hair. I'm not a baby anymore—I'm fifteen and old enough to wear my hair the way I want.* This last thought consoled her as she fell into a deep, exhausted sleep.

In the morning Cecilia kneaded the bread dough sullenly. She avoided Mamá's eye and kept silent while she did her chores. On the school bus, she fingered the scapular she wore around her neck. As soon as the weather became cooler, Mamá made each child wear a scapular around their necks. The scapular was made of two small square pieces of cloth sewn together to make a little pouch. The children wore it on a string instead of a chain. The cloth was embroidered with a cross or the figure of a saint. Mamá filled the small pouch with camphor crystals to ward off disease. The camphor had a strong, medicinal smell. Cecilia hated it. It embarrassed her to reek of camphor all day. What would the town girls think? She took the scapular off and put it in her lunch pail. She would put it on before going home. Mamá would never know.

Cecilia looked down at her hands and cringed. Her fingers were stained brown from all the pecans she had shelled last night. No amount of scrubbing could wash away the stains. Maybe it was better she wasn't going to the dance with her old-fashioned braids and her stained hands. And, anyway, Johnny wouldn't be there. *I miss him so much,* Cecilia thought. *Will I ever see him again?*

Cecilia sat looking out the bus window and feeling sorry for herself. The fall landscape was dull brown, and the trees stood half-bare, their leaves shriveled and dry. *I feel like one of those trees,* thought Cecilia. *Always trying to reach up to the sky, but like the leaves, falling down to the ground.*

ALTHOUGH CECILIA didn't get to go to the homecoming dance, she did have an exciting Friday at school. One of her wild Apodaca cousins let a mouse out in study hall. All the girls screamed and stood on their chairs while the boys whistled and yelled. The teacher was furious, but she too jumped up on her chair. Then in home economics, Cecilia and Loretta cooked a strange vegetable Cecilia had never seen before. It was called an artichoke and had spiky leaves over a layer of fuzz. Cecilia was surprised to find the heart of the artichoke was delicious. The girls also prepared a tuna casserole, which was a treat for Cecilia, as they never had canned tuna at home. And finally, in honor of homecoming, a choral group from the college in Las Cruces performed at an assembly. Cecilia sat mesmerized. She loved music, and she often sang at home while Elías played his guitar. The group sang a popular song, *Tumbling Tumbleweeds*, and Cecilia hoped Elías would learn to play it on his guitar so she could sing along.

On the bus, Belle took out the new Tangee lipstick she had bought at Busby's Drug Store in Hatch. She applied some to her lips and then put some on Cecilia.

"Look in the mirror," Belle said. She held up a pretty gold compact she had received from an admirer, Adrian Molina. It was engraved with the words, *"This will enhance your popularity."* Cecilia looked in the mirror and liked the way the tangerine color looked against her skin. But she didn't dare wear it home. She wiped it off with her handkerchief. Then she made a decision.

"Belle, I'm going over to your house in the morning. I want you to cut my hair like yours," Cecilia said. Belle squealed with delight.

"No, no! Be quiet! You must not say anything," Cecilia warned. "If Mamá finds out…"

"I won't tell a soul!" Belle said. "Oh, I can't wait! I know just how to do it. You're going to look so swanky!"

That night Cecilia lit a candle and knelt in front of the statue of the Virgin Mary. *"Virgencita*, please forgive me for what I am going to do tomorrow. And please make Mamá understand." She crawled into her bed, which was already warmed by Belia's sleeping figure, feeling a mixture of excitement and dread in her stomach.

True to her word, Belle gave Cecilia a simple, yet flattering haircut. The two long braids lay in Cecilia's lap as Belle snipped at stray strands of hair. Then she twisted Cecilia's damp hair into pincurls and secured them with bobby pins. The two cousins sat outside in the morning sun waiting for Cecilia's hair to dry.

"*Prima*, I have a secret. Do you promise not to tell?" Belle said. Cecilia had noticed all morning that Belle was even more vivacious and talkative than usual.

"*Te lo prometo*," Cecilia promised.

"Do you promise in the name of Santa Cecilia, your patron saint?" Belle insisted.

"*Sí, sí.* I promise!"

"Adrian Molina asked me to marry him!" Belle announced.

Cecilia was speechless with shock. All she could do was stare with eyes wide opened.

"Don't look at me that way. It's true. We want to get married," Belle said.

"Get married? But you're only 15!" Cecilia said.

"I'll be 16 soon. And Adrian is already 18. We're old enough. My mamá got married when she was 16. Why shouldn't I?" Belle said. It was true that many farm girls married young and didn't finish school. But the idea horrified Cecilia. Cutting her hair was a small act of rebellion, but getting married—that was too extreme!

"Oh, no, Belle! You can't! You're too young. You need to graduate. And there are so many things still to do," Cecilia said.

"We love each other. That's all that matters. Adrian is already working a section of his father's land. He can support us," Belle said. Cecilia wondered how her pampered cousin could be happy living as a farmer's wife.

"But my tío and tía would never let you—would they?" she asked.

Belle tossed her head. "It's not up to them. It's *my* life. Adrian says we can elope to Las Cruces or even El Paso. We'll be married before they can stop us."

"Oh, Belle, please think about it more. *Piénsalo bien.* It will be a terrible mistake. You should talk to Padre Arteta about it," Cecilia urged.

"Oh, what does *he* know about being in love and getting married? *I* know what *I* want. And don't you go tattling to Tía Sara or your mamá. Remember, you promised not to tell," Belle warned.

"I'll light a candle for you," Cecilia said. "You should light one, too, and say a prayer for guidance."

"Oh, you! You're always lighting candles and saying prayers! When are you going to grow up and think for yourself?" Belle laughed. She combed out Cecilia's hair. "Look!" she ordered. Cecilia looked into the small mirror Belle held up. Cecilia gasped. She was startled to see how different she looked—older and more modern. The curly bangs above her eyes made her face look less thin and narrow. She liked it!

If only Johnny could see her now! Would he like it too? Would he think she looked pretty? If only they could see each other again.

As Cecilia walked home, braids in her pocket, her head felt weightless with her new haircut. But she felt the heavy burden of Belle's secret on her chest. She had promised not to tell anyone. How could she change Belle's mind? What could she do to stop Belle from making a terrible mistake?

Cecilia walked into the kitchen, absorbed in her thoughts. Mamá and Tía Sara were sitting at the table drinking a midmorning *ponche*, a hot foamy drink made with eggs, milk, sugar, and cinnamon. Mamá needed extra nourishment to fortify herself for the birth of the baby. They looked up as Cecilia entered. Tía Sara took one look at Cecilia and immediately turned to see her sister's reaction. Mamá looked at Cecilia for a long time without speaking. Then she said, "How dare you cut your hair without my permission? *¿Cómo te atreves?*" The coldness of her tone sent a shiver down Cecilia's spine. She could tell Mamá was really angry. Cecilia stood silently without answering.

"*¡Contéstame!* Answer me!" Mamá demanded. Tía Sara looked down into her cup and pressed her lips together tightly. She wanted to intervene but knew this was between mother and daughter. Cecilia still stood silently. What could she say to her mother? Her braids were gone. She couldn't say she was sorry because she wasn't. She was glad she had cut them off, and she liked the way she looked. Why wouldn't

Mamá let her grow up? Cecilia raised her chin defiantly.

"Cecilia, I never expected this kind of behavior from you. From your cousin Belle, yes. But not you. And especially at this time when I am not well. This is what comes from letting you go to high school in town and being influenced by all those wild girls. All you are learning there is rebellion and disobedience. I am very disappointed in you." Mamá gripped the edge of the table and lifted herself up from her chair. She faced Cecilia.

"Your papá is getting things ready for the *matanza* next week. Tell Belia and the boys they won't be going to school Wednesday. They need to stay home and help. You will stay home from school for as long as I need you here to help in the kitchen and with the rendering of the lard. Now go to your room."

Cecilia didn't let her tears flow until she reached her bedroom. Then she threw herself across the bed and sobbed. How could Mamá be so old-fashioned, so unfeeling? She didn't seem to care about Cecilia's feelings or about her happiness at all. Now Cecilia would be forced to miss two or three days of school. She would have more makeup work than she could handle. How would she be able to maintain her A average? Her grades were sure to go down! She would be humiliated in front of her teachers and the other students who recognized her as an exceptional student. At least Johnny wouldn't be in school to see her humiliation. Cecilia thought about Belle and her plans to elope. Maybe Belle was right to want to get married and be independent. At least she would be living her own life and making her own decisions. Mamá didn't even want Cecilia to have control over her own hair! *If only I were older, I could marry Johnny and live in El Paso!*

"CECILIA! CECILIA! Come quickly. *¡Ven, ven!*" Belia shouted at Cecilia from the kitchen on Monday. Cecilia, just getting home from school, ran toward the door.

"¿Qué pasa? What happened? Is Mamá all right?" Cecilia asked in fear.

"A postcard came in the mail today! It's for you!" Belia said excitedly. The family rarely received mail. Now and then a letter came from a distant relative, so a postcard for Cecilia was a very exciting event.

"A postcard? For me?" Cecilia asked. She felt a sudden hot feeling in her stomach and her face began to flush. Could it be a card from Johnny? Had he finally remembered her after all this time? Cecilia could hardly wait to see the postcard.

"Here it is," said Belia as she handed her the small piece of cardboard bearing a two-cent stamp of George Washington.

Cecilia quickly glanced at the message. Her heart sank with disappointment. The postcard wasn't from Johnny. But then she brightened. It was from Miss May Malone! The front of the card showed a picture of the State Teachers College in Silver City, New Mexico, where Miss Malone was teaching now. On the back she had written, *"Dear Cecilia, how are you now? I'm in Silver City. Write me a long letter soon. Tell everyone hello. Love, Miss May."* She had included her new address. Cecilia clutched the postcard to her chest. She had never received anything in the mail in all her life. She would save this card forever! She could hardly wait to write Miss Malone a long letter telling her all about her high school classes. If it weren't for Miss Malone, she wouldn't even be in high school!

Cecilia went into the house to put down her books and help with supper. She had taken over more and more of Mamá's work so Mamá could rest. After doing her homework every night, she had little time to read for pleasure. Cecilia was desperate for some private time to be alone with her thoughts and to read her precious books. Right now she was in the middle of a wonderful novel, *Ramona*, by Helen Hunt Jackson, about a half-Indian girl raised as a Spaniard. It was the saddest and most romantic story she had ever read. Like Ramona, she felt frustrated and torn in two directions. On the one hand, she resented having to take over so many of Mamá's duties and having so little time for herself. Yet on the other hand, she genuinely looked forward to having a new brother or sister. She sympathized with poor Ramona who was torn between her Indian heritage and her Spanish upbringing. And she knew she loved Johnny the way Ramona loved Alessandro the Indian. *Why did things have to be so confusing? Why couldn't life be simple?* she wondered.

A *MATANZA* was a big event in the fall. Every year as soon as the weather turned cold, Papá slaughtered one of their pigs. The pig provided pork for *chorizo* sausage, bacon, ham, and the meat used in stews and *chile con carne*. But most importantly, the fat was rendered into *manteca*—lard—which was a vital staple in the kitchen. Lard was used for baking and frying everything they ate. The children even loved it spread on bread as an after-school snack. Besides its food value, lard was also used to grease farm equipment and to rub on rough, chapped skin. The solid white lard would be stored in coffee cans and would last all year until the next *matanza*.

A *matanza* was labor-intensive work that required the help of the entire family and anyone else who was willing to join in and be rewarded with a delicious meal afterwards. This year the Vetters would be helping, and as usual, Tío Santiago walked over with his wife and their children—Leo, Ray, Elena, and Junior—to join in the work. While Papá and Tío Santiago slaughtered the pig by piercing it in the heart with a sharp knife, the younger children hid under a bed. They hated to see one of their animals killed. Once the pig was hung from a tree, the children came out to carry pans back and forth between the slaughtering area and the kitchen. A large pan was placed under the pig to catch the blood as it drained. Mamá cooked the blood with sugar and raisins until it turned a dark, black color. No part of the pig was wasted. Tío Santiago even cut off the tail and ears and threw them onto hot coals to toast. The children fought over these crunchy treats.

The boys hauled buckets of water from the pump to fill a large barrel, which had been placed on a grate over a fire built in a pit. The water was heated to boiling. Then everyone used pots to pour the boiling water over the pig in order to loosen its hair. Papá had a special metal scraper, which he dragged over the pig's body, scraping off all the hair. Tío Santiago was an expert butcher. He used a sharp knife to cut the pig into its usable parts. The women waited in the kitchen for a tray of pork to begin cooking *chile verde con carne.* While they waited, they made the traditional blue corn tortillas made only for *matanzas* from corn grown on the farm.

Outside, the men cut the fat into small chunks, cooking them over a blazing fire to render the fat into lard. In another large cauldron, Papá made *chicharrones*—chunks of fat and pork fried crisp in lard. The crispy chunks were delicious eaten hot and wrapped in corn tortillas with a little salt. *Chicharrones* lasted a long time in the *dispensa*, the pantry off the kitchen, and were eaten for weeks. The children even took them in their school lunches. They loved to nibble on the tasty, crunchy chunks of meat. Mamá had the children deliver chunks of pork wrapped in paper to their neighbors and relatives who lived on surrounding farms. All day, the boys ran back and forth making deliveries.

Atole was the traditional drink during the *matanza.* Tía Sara made the thick drink by whisking hot water into cornmeal and flavoring it with milk, sugar, and vanilla. She served it piping hot in mugs to the men outside. Tía Sara was an expert in whisking *atole*. Hers was never lumpy like the *atole* of some of Cecilia's other aunts.

When all the work was done, the men washed up at the pump and came into the warm kitchen where the women had been cooking all morning. Everyone sat down to an enormous meal of *chile verde con carne, frijoles de la olla,* a *sopita* of rice, and blue corn tortillas. There was even a big pot of *verdolagas,* or wild purslane, that the children had found in the fields yesterday. Mamá had fried them with onions and tomatoes. For dessert Mamá served her homemade peach pie and hot, fragrant coffee. Everything was delicious!

That night everyone went to bed early from exhaustion. They had all worked very hard to get a necessary job done. The family had worked together and eaten together, along with their new friends from Oklahoma. In fact, the Vetters were almost like family now. Cecilia lay in her bed listening to Jeannie Vetter's quiet breathing as she slept on a mat on the floor. She loved Jeannie like a sister. Mr. Vetter had saved up quite a bit of money and was fixing up his car. Cecilia knew they would be leaving in a few days. She didn't want them to go. She and Jeannie had so many plans, so many things they wanted to do together. Jeannie had spent every day reading Cecilia's books and could read anything now. Cecilia was so proud of her!

Why does time go so fast? Cecilia thought. It seemed as if the Vetters had just arrived here in their old jalopy, looking tired and underfed. Now they were all robust and rested, and their father was ready to take them to a new life in California. *Why do things have to change? Why can't good things last forever?* she wondered. But she knew the answers to those questions. It was all a part of life and of growing up.

As Cecilia had feared, four days later, the Vetters were ready to ride on down the road. The old car was fixed and now sat with boxes and suitcases tied to the roof and to its sides. Mamá had filled baskets with food for their journey— dried fruit, bread, beef jerky, and of course, *chicharrones*. Everyone gathered on the porch to say goodbye, and all the women and girls were crying. Belia's dog Chata and the Vetter's dog Jeep, jumped all over everyone and turned circles in the excitement. Jeep was staying behind. He and Chata had become such good friends that the Vetters didn't have the heart to separate them. Besides, the long trip across the desert would be hard enough without worrying about a dog.

Cecilia and Jeannie moved away from the others. "I have a present for you to remember me by," said Jeannie. She held out a beautiful snow globe. Inside the ball of glass was a sailboat floating in water. As Cecilia shook the globe, little white flecks snowed down on the boat. "It's the best thing I have," said Jeannie. "I want you to have it."

"Oh, Jeannie, how beautiful! I'll treasure it forever! Here, this is for you." Cecilia held out something wrapped in brown paper. Jeannie unwrapped the gift and pulled out the azure dress Cecilia had made in home economics class. It was a beautiful dress with a small cape that buttoned at the neck.

"Oh, Cecilia! Your dress! Do you really want me to have it?" cried Jeannie.

"Of course I do!" said Cecilia. "I made it myself, so every time you wear it, you'll remember me."

"Oh, Cecilia, I could never forget you. You're my best friend. This is the most beautiful dress I've ever had!" The two girls began to cry as they hugged each other and said goodbye. Jeannie whispered in Cecilia's ear, "Johnny will come back. I know he will. He could never forget you either."

"*Adiós,* goodbye!" everyone shouted at once. Mr. Vetter turned the key in the ignition and the old car started smoothly. As he drove away, a half dozen hands reached out the car windows, waving goodbye. Tía Sara waved her handkerchief. Everyone stood on the porch until the car disappeared around a bend in the road.

"*Que Dios les bendiga,*" said Mamá. "May God bless them."

CHAPTER 5

Quien bien te quiere te hará llorar.

The one who loves you well will make you cry.

Life on the farm was dull without the Vetters. Cecilia thought about Jeannie everyday and wondered if the family had made it to California without their old jalopy breaking down again. Every night before she went to sleep she picked up the snow globe Jeannie had given her and shook it. She watched the "snow" fall down around the little ship in the center of the glass ball and imagined she was on that ship sailing to an exciting port. But here she was instead on a little farm tucked away in a quiet Rio Grande valley hemmed in by tall purple mountains, while Jeannie was in sunny California seeing new and exciting things.

For a moment Cecilia envied her. Then she thought of Papá and Mamá and the new baby coming, and she knew she wouldn't trade places with anybody. She loved Papá with

103

his bristly black mustache and gentle personality. And even though Mamá was strict and unbending, she was also strong and loving. Cecilia loved her mother. But it hurt her that Mamá couldn't understand and respect Cecilia's dreams and goals. Cecilia was happiest when she was reading and studying. She looked forward to a future life working in a big city, earning money and helping Papá pay the farm mortgage and all the other bills he worried over so much. *If only Mamá could see that I am different from her, that I want different things,* Cecilia thought. Ever since the day Cecilia cut her hair, she and Mamá had spoken very little to each other. They went about their daily duties quietly, with Tía Sara looking on anxiously.

Cecilia hoped Jeannie had enrolled in school in her new home. She wondered what school was like in California. She loved her own high school and was thrilled to be a Hatch Bear, the school mascot. Yesterday had been a good day at school. She was sewing a brown wool suit in home economics class, and she had impressed Miss Gustafson with her hand-stitched buttonholes. In algebra class, when Mr. Fox had asked who had their homework, Cecilia had been the only student to raise her hand. Mr. Fox had asked her to write the problems on the blackboard and explain them to the class. He had given her twenty extra credit points! After class, Mr. Fox had told her she was a fine student and he was very proud of her. If only Mamá could be proud of her success at school as well.

Cecilia buttoned her coat and tied her knitted scarf tighter around her head. She was walking to the Iglesia de

San Isidro to say confession so she could take holy communion at mass tomorrow morning. But more ugently, she wanted to talk to Padre Arteta about Belle and her impending elopement. Her worries about Belle had taken her mind off her own troubles for a while. She had been worried sick about Belle running off to marry Adrian. She was powerless to stop Belle from making this mistake. Adrian was handsome, hardworking and well-mannered, but Belle was too young to be married!

The worst part was she had to keep the knowledge to herself. There was no one Cecilia could talk to. She couldn't even tell Tía Sara, in whom she usually confided her secrets. Tía Sara was Belle's aunt as well, and she may have been able to help. But Cecilia had promised Belle she wouldn't tell anyone, and she had to keep her word. But Padre Arteta was different. He was a priest. Talking to him in the confessional was like talking to God. And besides, Cecilia felt comfortable with Padre Arteta. She had known him all her life. He had even baptized her when she was born.

A sharp, cold wind blew down her neck even though she clutched the collar of her coat tightly under her chin. Winter had been unusually cold this year. Snow had already fallen twice this month. The cottonwood trees that lined the dirt road had lost all their leaves to the frost. Now they stood with bare spidery limbs dotted with clusters of mistletoe. The mistletoe made Cecilia think of Johnny. If he were here, they might have been able to kiss under the mistletoe at a Christmas dance when no one was watching.

The thought of kissing Johnny made her blush, and she could feel her face getting warm in spite of the cold wind. No one had any news of Johnny, and he hadn't written to anyone—not even her. Cecilia had stopped asking about him. She was afraid her friends would discover her feelings for him. He probably didn't even remember her anymore. He probably had lots of girlfriends in El Paso. He had kissed her and then forgotten all about her. *Stop moping!* she ordered herself.

She pushed thoughts of Johnny out of her mind. This was not the time to be thinking of him. She had to hurry to the church and accomplish her mission before the sun went down, otherwise she would be walking home in the dark. And those black clouds above looked ominous. She didn't want to get caught in the rain. She peered up at the sky. High above her, a flock of birds floated like ships sailing on a gray sea. On the ground, her shoes made crunching sounds on the dry, crusty clay of the road. Rain would be welcomed today—but only after she got home!

A sudden clap of thunder startled her. Walking into the wind with her head down, she tried to pick up her pace. She reached the church and went inside, thankful for its silence. The church was only slightly warmer than the air outside. Several people were kneeling in the pews with their heads bent in prayer. Candles burned in front of the statues of the Virgin Mary and San Isidro, the patron saint of farmers. San Isidro was an important saint for this community, and the people prayed to him for better weather for their crops—for more rain or for less rain depending on what time of the year it was. They prayed to him to keep their farm animals healthy. They prayed for him to stop blight, fungus, and boll weevil from killing their crops. Their prayers were heartfelt and important, for the success of their crops was necessary to their survival.

Cecilia curtseyed and crossed herself in front of the altar. She went inside the empty confessional and drew the curtain across the entrance of the small booth.

"Bless me, Father, for I have sinned," she began. "My last confession was seven days ago." She confessed to Padre Arteta all her transgressions of the week, which amounted to not much more than having had disobedient thoughts and being short-tempered with her brothers. Then she told him about Belle's and Adrian's plans for an elopement.

"Padre, I'm so worried. I don't know what to do. I've tried to change her mind, but she won't listen. She's going to make a terrible mistake!" Cecilia said.

"Cecilia, you are a good cousin to Belle. It is right that you are concerned about her and want to help her. But you cannot take all the troubles of the world on your shoulders. That is not God's plan for us. You must put your trust in your prayers. God will hear you. Encourage Belle to pray, too, and to ask for God's guidance. You must also trust your cousin to do the right thing. Remember, God is watching over her, too," Padre Arteta explained. "Now go say five Hail Marys and get home before the storm breaks."

Cecilia knelt down in a pew next to Doña Carlota. The smell of camphor and coal oil reeked from the tiny woman's clothing. Doña Carlota wore a soiled white scarf around her head and many layers of clothing in an attempt to stave off the cold. As usual, she wore all her clothing inside out. She mumbled in prayer as she fingered the beads of a rosary held between her rough, brown hands.

Doña Carlota was very old and very eccentric. She lived by herself in a hut down the road. When Cecilia was younger, she had been fascinated by the old woman's dress and mannerisms. Once Cecilia had sat next to her during mass. When the collection plate was passed, Doña Carlota had pulled out a soiled handkerchief, which was knotted into a pouch. She had carefully untied the knot with her gnarled fingers, and Cecilia had caught a glimpse of three pennies in the center of the handkerchief. Very carefully, Doña Carlota had picked out one penny and had put it into the collection basket. Now, Cecilia smiled shyly at her as she knelt to say her penance.

Cecilia left the church with a lighter heart. Padre Arteta was wise and what he said must be true. If she couldn't change Belle's mind, she would encourage her to pray for guidance. And she herself would pray to God to watch over Belle and protect her. She walked home quickly through a light sprinkle. By the time she reached the kitchen door, rain was pouring down. The kitchen was warm and welcoming. Mamá was brewing a fresh pot of coffee.

"Cecilia, go to my *ropero* and bring me my shawl. I think it is on the top shelf," Mamá said.

Cecilia went to Mamá's bedroom and opened the heavy door to the tall, wide wardrobe that stood against one wall. Mamá had made the wardrobe herself out of planks of wood and had painted it a pale blue. She was a talented woman, and carpentry was only one of her many abilities. Cecilia reached up to feel for the shawl, but the shelf was too high. She stepped on the bottom of the wardrobe and with both hands grabbed the top shelf and tried to lift herself up. Suddenly the entire wardrobe fell on top of Cecilia, knocking her down and pinning her to the floor underneath. She was engulfed in all the clothes that had been hanging on the rod and was trapped beneath the entire weight of the heavy piece of furniture. She couldn't breathe! She felt as if she was suffocating! She tried to yell but couldn't get her breath, and the clothes and blankets that smothered her also muffled her cries. Just as she was about to pass out, the wardrobe was lifted off her.

"*¡Hija, hija! ¿Qué te pasó? ¡Pobrecita, mi hija!*"

Cecilia heard Mamá's frantic voice as from a distance.

"Cecilia, wake up! Wake up!" Mamá cried as she lifted up Cecilia's head. Cecilia managed to sit up with Mamá's help. She felt dizzy and her head hurt. Tía Sara was there too, holding a bottle of strong-smelling ammonia under Cecilia's nose. The fumes of the ammonia roused her, but they also burned her nose and made her head ache worse.

"*¿Qué pasó?* What happened?" Tía Sara asked as she rubbed Cecilia's hands. "We heard a crash and came running!" The two women had somehow managed to lift the heavy *ropero* off Cecilia.

Cecilia drank a few sips of water from the glass Tía Sara held to her lips. "The *ropero* fell on me. I couldn't breathe!" She whimpered from the shock.

"*Pobrecita, pobrecita. Descansa aquí.* Rest here on my bed until supper," Mamá said. And Mamá sat on the bed with Cecilia's head in her lap while she caressed her forehead and crooned, "*Descansa, descansa. Todo está bien.* Just rest, everything is fine." Cecilia wasn't used to her mother treating her like this. Mamá was always so busy cooking and cleaning for the children that she didn't have time to be affectionate. For the first time since Cecilia had cut her hair, Mamá spoke warmly and lovingly to her. Cecilia lay still, enjoying the feel of her mother's cool hand on her forehead. *Mamá must love me after all,* she thought before her eyes closed again. She must have dozed off. When she woke up, Belia was sitting by the bed.

"Can you come eat supper now? Mamá didn't have time to cook because of your accident. She sat by you all afternoon while you slept. So Papá gave me a quarter to buy five cans of sardines from the store. We're going to have sardines and crackers for supper!" Belia said. "Come on before the boys eat them all!"

At the supper table, Cecilia smiled shyly at everyone. She

felt embarrassed about her accident, and she was still feeling wobbly. She said, "I saw Doña Carlota at the church today."

"*Pobre mujer.* Poor woman. She has had a hard life," said Mamá. "Tomorrow I'll send her some *empanadas.* Fito, you and Roberto can take them after church."

Fito and Roberto looked at each other nervously. They didn't want to go to Doña Carlota's house. She was a witch! *¡Una bruja!* All the children went out of their way to avoid passing her strange little house. Now Mamá was ordering them to actually go to the witch's house! Mamá would never believe them if they tried to tell her Doña Carlota was a witch. Fito and Roberto poked each other under the table, but they knew it was no use to argue with Mamá. Besides, they could eat a few of the *empanadas* themselves on the way. No one would ever know.

"How is my birthday girl?" Papá said as he pulled Sylvia onto his lap after he had finished eating. She would be three years old in a few days. Sylvia put her arms around his neck and licked his cheek. She liked the salty taste of the sweat that had dried on his face. Papá took her little hand in his and holding each finger one at a time, recited her favorite finger rhyme.

> "*Cinco pollitos*
> *Tiene mi tía;*
> *Uno le canta,*
> *Uno le pía,*
> *Y tres le tocan la chirimía.*"

"Five little chickies

Has my aunt;

One sings to her,

One cheeps to her,

And three play the flute for her."

Sylvia giggled and said *"Otra vez."* She always wanted him to play the game over and over again.

"I finished making a chair for Sylvia today," Mamá said. She went into the pantry and came back out carrying a child-sized wooden chair. Stained brown, it had a tall, straight back and was a miniature version of the chairs that stood around the parlor table. It was exactly the right size for a little girl, and Mamá had made it herself! Sylvia slid off Papá's lap and sat in the chair. She crossed her chubby little legs like an adult and everyone burst out laughing. "My chair," she said. *"Es mi silla."*

"There's a writing contest at school," Cecilia said. "Whoever writes the best short story will win five dollars. I want to enter it. I have an idea for a story."

"Just make sure you do all your chores first," Mamá said.

"Mamá, I *always* do my chores!" Cecilia said. Mamá had hurt her feelings by implying that Cecilia might shirk her duties. When would Mamá appreciate everything Cecilia did? When would she come to accept Cecilia's love of school and learning? *Why does Mamá always treat me like this? No matter what I do, it's never enough,* Cecilia thought.

As if reading Cecilia's mind, Tía Sara said, "Cecilia always works hard. I'm sure she can write a wonderful story. Cecilia, I know you can win the contest."

"Well, if she wins the contest we can use the money because the midwife is charging us five dollars to deliver the baby," said Mamá.

"No!" said Papá sternly, slamming down his coffee mug on the table. Everyone was startled at the tone of his voice. Papá rarely spoke in such a serious way. "If my daughter wins the contest, she will keep her money. She will have earned it. I will pay for my child's birth. It is not her responsibility."

Cecilia felt a thrill of pride in her father. He had come to her defense! He had stood up to Mamá, which he rarely did, especially when it came to handling the girls in the family. She knew *he* at least was proud of her and her accomplishments. She also knew deep in her heart that Papá loved her the best of all his children.

"*Si tú lo puedes imaginar, tú lo puedes alcanzar,*" said Tía Sara, smoothing things over. "Cecilia, you know you can achieve anything you want if you have faith and work hard enough."

THAT NIGHT after all her chores were done, after all the dishes were washed and put away, after all the children were tucked into bed, and the house was dark and quiet, Cecilia stayed up long after midnight, writing by the meager light of a coal oil lamp. She wrote on a ruled tablet with a thick pencil Elías had sharpened for her with his knife. She titled her story *Dick Rowel's Luck*. It was a story about a cattle rancher and his loving daughter Betty who were about to lose their ranch due to cattle theft. Dick Rowel, Betty's admirer, risked his life to catch the thieves, and Betty, in a daring rescue, came to his aid. Cecilia named her heroine Betty after Betty Zane, the brave heroine in one of Cecilia's favorite books. And hadn't her family almost lost their own farm to the bank last year? Cecilia licked the point of her pencil and wrote her name proudly on the cover sheet. Then she began to write:

DICK ROWEL'S LUCK

In a small house fifteen miles from the gambling town of Gila, Mr. Jones and his daughter Betty waited in suspense for Mr. Smith to return.

"Dad, do you think Mr. Smith will really take this house away from us?"

"I hope he doesn't, Betty, but if we only knew what became of our cattle we could keep the place, there's ninety-five head of cattle and Smith told me he wanted to buy them."

"In the morning I am going to see if Dick Rowel will help me find them," said Betty as she gave a long sigh.

"But, daughter, I don't want you to do that; it is a man's job," said her father.

"Yes, but your troubles are mine, Dad," she said as she went up to his chair.

A knock was heard at the door. Mr. Jones got up to answer it.

"Come in, Smith, have a chair."

"No, thanks. I haven't time. Jones, I came over

to claim the place. I give you until Saturday to get out, goodbye."

"Oh, Dad, maybe between now and then we can find our cattle so we can pay him."

"Let's go to bed now, Betty, and we will talk it over tomorrow."

Betty kissed her father and went to her room, but not to bed. She changed into her riding suit, took her gun, and slipped out to the corrals. She saddled her pony, Tex, and went silently by the house.

"Come on, Tex, we have work to do tonight. Here is a trail of a herd of cattle leading to the York's place; let's follow it." Tex started in a long run and his shoe clicked against something. Betty got off and picked up an object. It was Dick Rowel's spur.

"So Dick is in that gang too; I should tell Dad but I better follow the trail."

She saw that her gun was all right and started down the trail taking all cautions possible. She went on through a pass and around a bend to a secret valley where she saw a herd of cattle. She got off, slapping Tex, and took him up behind a bush.

"Now you stay here and when I whistle you better come out."

Tex shook his head as if to say yes. Betty started-ed crouching toward a light which shone through a small window. It came from a cave where some men were talking.

As she neared the opening she heard Dick groaning and saying that he wouldn't say anything if they turned him loose. As the three men were about to place a torch to Dick's foot, Betty entered pointing her gun at them.

"Stick them up, you three. Dick come nearer, I'll untie you."

"Gee! I am surely glad you came. How did you find me? Did you find my spur?"

"Yes, how came you to be with them? Now let's take these boys over to the sheriff and also take the cattle back. We will all go together. You take the boys and I'll drive the cattle."

They all walked in silence toward the Jones's place. As they were nearing the house they met Mr. Jones. He had heard all the noise and gone out to see what it was. As soon as Betty saw her father she ran up to him telling him that they could keep the house now.

"Mr. Jones, here is the cattle and the York gang; you can have them," said Dick.

"All right, Dick, and I'll give you the old model T as a wedding present."

"Dick, tell me how came you to lose your spur," asked Betty.

"Oh, let that go. I'll tell you later; right now I am starving for food...and your kisses."

"You will have to wait until I cook supper, but here is your kiss."

THE END

THAT NIGHT a light snow fell over the valley. In the morning, the snowy fields lay varnished in the thin sunshine that filtered down through the clouds. By afternoon, only a few wisps of clouds remained in the sky and all the snow had melted. *Nothing ever lasts,* Cecilia thought. *Everything is always changing. Even the snow is already gone.*

As she opened the door to the kitchen, Fito and Roberto almost knocked her down.

"¡Cuidado!" Be careful!" she said. Fito was carrying a plate of *empanadas* that they were taking to Doña Carlota. "Behave yourselves with Doña Carlota," she warned her little brothers. She knew what all the children thought about the poor old woman.

"Cecilia, Juanito Apodaca says she is a witch!" said Fito. "It's true! He says she is really the Empress Carlota of Mexico—the one who was married to the Emperor Maximiliano. That's why she has the same name. He says she went crazy after he was executed by the firing squad. She is still alive and hiding here, and she won't ever die because she is a witch."

"No digas eso. Don't talk such nonsense. If Mamá hears you, she'll hit you with the *chicote.* Doña Carlota is a *curandera.* She is not a witch. She helps people with their problems. She makes them well again. Don't you tease her like the other boys," Cecilia said. "They're always throwing rocks at her house."

"No, no. We'll leave the *empanadas* and run back home," said Roberto, looking up at his sister with brown eyes opened wide in fear.

"Well, don't be late for supper. I'm helping Mamá make *albóndigas,"* Cecilia said.

"Mmmm!" the boys cried. They loved the hot, spicy meatball soup Mamá only made in the winter. They raced off to complete their errand.

In the kitchen, Cecilia put a pot of water to boil on the

stove. Mamá had already ground a piece of meat using her hand grinder. Cecilia chopped onion and garlic and threw them into the pot. Then she mixed the ground meat with rice and dried *cilantro*. The herb was aromatic and filled the kitchen with its delicious smell. Mamá came in to check on Cecilia's work.

"Don't forget what I've taught you. *Bueno es cilantro, pero no tanto*. Cilantro is good, but don't overdo it." She was silent for a moment. Then she said, "It is a good lesson for your life as well," Mamá said. "You are always worrying about your schoolwork and spending too much time with your books. You are always wasting time dreaming about things that are not going to happen. You expect too much out of life. Cecilia, *hija*, I wish you could be satisfied and accept things the way they are. I am afraid you will only be disappointed."

"Mamá, why can't you understand me? Why don't you have faith in me and what I can do? Tía Sara and Papá do. Why are you the only one who discourages me from making a better life for myself? What is so wrong about wanting to get a job in the city, to earn money, to see new places?" Cecilia said, tears brimming in her eyes.

"I want you to have a good life. And you can make a good life here, like I did. A girl should stay with her family until she has a family of her own. There are plenty of good young men here for you to choose from. A decent girl does not talk about going to a city and living alone as you want to do. *No es decente*," Mamá said.

"*¡Sí soy decente!*" Cecilia cried. "I am not like some of the other girls who are always looking out their windows to see the boys passing by. Some of the town girls ride in cars alone with their boyfriends. They even lie to their parents and go all the way to Juárez on Saturday nights. I don't do those things. All I want is to see more than just a farm everyday, to do more than just cook and clean and wash clothes. I want to see the rest of the world! There is so much more out there. Why can't you understand?"

"I understand that you think our life here isn't good enough for you!" Mamá said angrily as she stormed out of the kitchen. Cecilia was stunned. How could Mamá think such a thing? Mamá didn't understand her at all! She would never understand!

Would she and Mamá ever stop arguing over the same thing? Cecilia wondered as she tried to keep her tears from falling into the pot of *albóndigas*.

While Cecilia and her mother were arguing, Fito and Roberto were approaching Doña Carlota's house. Her house was a tiny *jacal* made of adobe with wooden poles and sticks forming a roof. The eccentric old woman had surrounded her house with dried brush, piles of rocks, and bits and pieces of coiled wire she had scavenged in her wanderings. Sticks and poles leaned against the shack as if propping up its walls.

The boys walked carefully—everyone knew Doña Carlota had booby traps all around her house. She had dug holes, camouflaging them with piles of dried brush and tangles of vines. As they approached the house timidly, the door creaked open and Doña Carlota stood on her doorstep. She must have seen them coming from one of her tiny windows. Fito thrust the plate of *empanadas* at her, and without saying a word, the two boys ran toward home as fast as they could.

The next Saturday afternoon, Tío Santiago and his family walked over for a visit. Fito and Roberto told their cousins Leo and Ray all about their visit to Doña Carlota's hut.

"When she opened her door, we could see inside. There were cats all over! And she was wearing her clothes inside out! And she had chile seeds stuck on her forehead!" said Fito.

"And she looked at me with her eyes crossed!" said Roberto. "That means she's a witch, a *bruja!* We ran away before she could do something to us!"

"Scaredy cats!" taunted Leo. "I wouldn't have run. I would have been brave enough to go inside her house. They say nobody has ever been inside."

"I dare you to go look inside her house!" said Fito. "Let's see how brave you are!"

"I'm braver than you are!" insisted Leo.

"Me, too," said Ray.

"I double dare you to look inside her window!" Fito said.

"Me, too," said Roberto.

"All right. Let's see who is the bravest. We'll all go and see who gets closest to her window and who runs away first," Leo challenged.

The four boys slipped away unnoticed in the dusk of the winter afternoon. They walked briskly to Doña Carlota's shack. As they approached it, they slowed their pace. Leo raised his two hands in the direction of the hut. He held his middle and ring fingers down with his thumb, his index and little finger pointing out like the horns of a cow. He told the other boys to make the same gesture with their fingers.

"This is how you keep witches away," he explained. The boys crept forward. The strange-looking hut loomed before them in the shadowy light. Who would be the first to run back home? As they inched closer, fingers outstretched to ward off evil, they forgot all about the boobytraps around the house. Just as Roberto, the bravest of them, was about to sneak up to a window, Leo tripped on a wire. He let out a cry as he fell to the ground with a thud. Roberto turned around to see what had happened and plunged into a deep hole underneath the window. He seemed to disappear right before their eyes! The terrified boys ran off into the darkness, leaving Roberto to his fate. Poor Roberto! He had scraped his hands and torn his pants as he slid into the hole.

"Help! Help!" he screamed. But the other boys had run far beyond the sound of his voice.

Suddenly a face appeared above him. It was Doña Carlota! She held up a lantern to see him better. The flickering light of the lantern lit up only her face and gave it the appearance of being suspended in the air without a body. Roberto screamed.

"¿Niño, qué haces aquí? ¿Porqué gritas? What are you doing here? Why are you screaming?" She reached out a hand and pulled him out of the hole by the back of his overalls. He stood speechless before her, trembling in terror. His feet were rooted to the ground in fear. Her grip was too strong for such an old lady! She *must* be a witch!

"Look at your face! It is scratched and bleeding! And your hands!" She took one of his hands in her old bony one and inspected it by the light of the lantern. *"¡Mira nomás!"* she said, clucking her tongue. "Come inside. I will clean your cuts and put some ointment on them." She took him firmly by the shoulders and pushed him into her house. The door was so low that it barely cleared Roberto's head. But the stooped old woman passed through easily.

All the stories he had heard about witches and young children rushed through his head. He had read stories about Hansel and Gretel in school. They had been put into a cage by a witch who wanted to fatten them up and eat them. The other boys had told him tales of *brujas* who kidnapped children and turned them into animals or strange creatures. What would she do to him? Would she turn him into a frog or a pig or even cook him for her supper? Roberto steeled himself to meet his fate.

CHAPTER 6

Caras vemos, corazones no sabemos.

Faces we see, hearts we don't know.

D oña Carlota nudged Roberto through the door of her tiny hut. The light from her lantern and from the fire that burned in her small fireplace cast strange, dancing shadows on the walls. Roberto stood in awe as he looked around him. He had never seen anything like this house. Hundreds of bundles of dried herbs hung from the rafters, and the mixture of their aromas filled the air along with the strong smells of camphor and coal oil. In the dim light he could see four or five cats sprawled on the few pieces of furniture in the room. They paid no attention to Roberto, although one of them eyed him suspiciously through slanted yellow eyes before going back to its nap.

But what impressed Roberto the most were the crucifixes. Crosses made of straw, dried palm leaves, twigs, sticks, paper, foil, and wire hung on every wall and in every corner of the room. Tiny silver crosses hung over the two small windows and over the doorway. As his eyes grew accustomed to the dim light in the room, he realized the crosses were made of needles. He had heard that witches wouldn't go through the eye of a needle, or even over one or under one. Why would Doña Carlota have them in her house? Wasn't she supposed to be a witch?

"*Siéntate, niño.* Sit down and I will fix you a nice tea to calm your nerves," she said. He sat in the only chair not occupied by a cat and continued to stare around the room, not saying a word. Doña Carlota brought out a mug and poured dried yellow leaves into it. She picked up a kettle that had been sitting on a grate in her fireplace and poured boiling water over the leaves. Roberto smelled the sweet, fragrant aroma of *flor de manzanilla*. Mamá always brewed the family chamomile tea when they were sick or couldn't sleep. Only a little suspicious, he drank a gulp of the hot liquid.

"Now, let me clean your scratches," Doña Carlota said. She filled a bowl with hot water and dipped a piece of cloth into it. She gently cleaned his hands and face with the warm cloth, wiping away the dirt, blood and tears. Roberto sat meekly. He was actually enjoying the warmth of the room and the soothing feel of the warm water on his skin and the hot drink in his stomach.

"What were you doing outside my house?" she asked bluntly.

Roberto was ashamed. He could see now that Doña Carlota was just a harmless old woman, an *abuelita*, like all the other old women in the community. He told the truth.

"We thought you were a *bruja*. The boys dared me to look in your window. I fell into a hole and they left me!" he said. Now that he was calm and not so afraid, he felt indignant at his brother's and cousins' abandonment of him. They thought she was a witch, and they had run off and left him in the hole!

"*¡Jesús, María, y José!* A witch! *No, no soy una bruja,*" she said. "But I know there *are* witches out there. I keep them from entering my house by growing gourds around my property. Witches hate the smell of gourds. And they won't cross my threshold because they fear the cross. That is why I have crucifixes all over as well."

"Then why do you wear your clothes inside out, and why do you have chile seeds on your forehead?" Roberto asked, curiosity getting the better of him.

Doña Carlota shooed a cat off a chair and sat down next to Roberto. "Don't you know that wearing your clothes inside out or backwards keeps witches away? And I put chile seeds on my forehead to cure my headaches. *¡Ay, qué muchachito!* Don't you know I am a *curandera*, a healer? People come to me for *remedios* for their ailments and other problems, and I help them. That is why I have all these *yerbas* and potions." She pointed at a row of small glass bottles standing on a shelf. "I have cures for everything—stomach trouble, toothache, coughs, rashes, burns, *gripa,* and even love sickness. The *té de manzanilla* you are drinking now will calm your nerves. You had a big fright."

"My mother passes an egg over her head when she has a headache," Roberto offered.

"That can work, too. But chile seeds are better. Tell your mamá I said so," Doña Carlota advised. Of course, Roberto had no intention of telling Mamá anything. She would whip him if she knew what he had done.

"What is that?" Roberto cried in fear. He pointed to a strange-looking statue sitting on a table. It had been carved from wood in the shape of a person and had something that looked like real human hair on its head.

"Don't you like my statue of Santa Bárbara? A *santero* in Santa Fé made it for me many years ago," she said. "Santa Bárbara helps protect my house. *Nadie se acuerda de Santa Bárbara hasta que truena.* No one thinks of Santa Bárbara until they are frightened by thunder. But I am always prepared. I have taken all these precautions ever since I saw a ball of fire fly over my little house one night. That is how witches travel, you know."

Roberto's fascinated eyes never left her face as she continued.

"Witches can change themselves into anything, into any form, and sneak into your house. My cats keep all the birds and mice away. You never know when a witch has turned herself into one of those creatures! Once a man came to me for help because he had been having bad luck. His crops had failed, his cows were dying of a strange illness, and his wife had left him. I asked him if he had noticed any small creatures hanging around his house. He said there had been a large black crow living in one of his trees. He could hear it cawing all night, and once he saw a flash of light in the tree. He thought the tree was on fire!"

"What did you do?" asked Roberto.

"I told him to get a bullet and cut a cross into it. I told him to take his gun and shoot the crow with that bullet. He did, and the crow fell to the ground, and you know what happened?" she asked, staring at him right in the eyes.

Roberto shook his head.

"The crow burst into flames when it hit the ground, and its black feathers turned into black ashes. The man's luck turned. His cows got well, and his wife came back to him. I know how to handle witches," she added with pride.

Doña Carlota leaned closer to Roberto and studied his face. "You look a lot like my son Juan. He was about your age when he died. He was a beautiful child with thick black curls and bright eyes. He had the happiest smile in our village. But one day a visitor passing through noticed him and complimented me on his beauty. The very next day Juan developed a fever and got sicker and sicker until he died. That visitor gave him the evil eye. *Le hizo el mal ojo,*" she explained. "I tried curing him by passing an egg over his body and burying it under a tree where the sun could not reach it. But he died anyway," she ended sadly.

Roberto knew all about *el mal ojo*. If anyone praised you or envied you too much, even unknowingly, people said "*Le hicieron el mal ojo.*" That is why Mamá didn't like her children bringing attention to themselves. He remembered a time when he had *soyamo* on his lip. Mamá had seen his fever blisters and told him to rub water on his head. But he had been worried because Mamá had told Tía Sara, "*Ójala que no le hicieron el mal ojo.*"

"My husband died when he was kicked by a horse. I have had an unlucky life," Doña Carlota sighed. "Now I try to help people with my potions and herbs. They give me a little food, some cloth, or a few pennies in exchange. I get by. Be a good boy and come back tomorrow and pump some water for me. Maybe you could chop some kindling for my little fire, too."

"Yes, I will do that. I promise I will come tomorrow and other days when I have a chance," Roberto said. He knew she wouldn't speak of this to Mamá and he was grateful. He also felt sorry for the old woman they had all misjudged. He would make sure the other boys never threw rocks at her house again.

WHEN ROBERTO returned home late with his arms and face scratched, he expected to be confronted by Mamá. She would surely demand to know where he had been so late. What he didn't expect was to find the entire household in an uproar. No one paid any attention to him at all. Mamá had gone into labor. She was having the baby!

Tía Sara herded all the children into their bedrooms and told them to stay there. They gathered in Cecilia's room, and Cecilia and Elías tried to keep them entertained. Elías played his guitar while Cecilia led them in the songs they all loved, such as *Cielito Lindo* and *El Rancho Grande*. Cecilia held Sylvia in her lap as she recited a riddle for the others to guess.

> *"De doce hermanos que somos*
> *El segundo yo nací.*
> *Pero soy el más pequeño,*
> *¿Cómo puede ser así?"*

> "Of twelve children born
> The second one was me.
> But I am the smallest,
> How can that be?"

No one could guess the answer to the riddle. "It's February!" cried Cecilia, and they all laughed and made her recite it again.

The midwife, Doña Telésfora, had been sent for and was taking care of Mamá in her room. Papá sat in the kitchen, drinking cup after cup of coffee. Even after having six children, he was still nervous about babies being born. Tía Sara went back and forth from Mamá's bedroom to the kitchen, giving Papá any news. After several hours, the baby had still not come. Papá was anxious and scared. He was worried about his wife's health and that of the baby. He didn't care if it was a boy or a girl, just as long as it was healthy. An hour later, Tía Sara stood in the doorway. "You now have eight children!" she announced.

"Eight? But how? *¿Pero cómo?*" Papá asked, confused. He only had six children up till now.

"You have twin daughters!" Tía Sara exclaimed. "*¡Son gemelas!*"

The family was delighted with the twin girls. After Fito and Belia were born, Papá never imagined he and Mamá would have a second set of twins. Mamá and both girls were healthy, although Mamá was weak. Twins! No wonder this pregnancy had been so difficult for Mamá. According to the custom of the time, she would have to stay in bed for forty days before she could resume her normal activities or even take a bath. This period of time was known as *la dieta*. Cecilia and Tía Sara would share the burden of Mamá's duties while she rested and regained her strength.

"What shall we name them?" Mamá asked Papá. "I would like one to be called 'Sara' after my sister."

Papá nodded and said, "And I would like the other to be named 'Celia' after Cecilia and Belia together." Cecilia and Belia were delighted with the babies' names. They were flattered that Mamá and Papá combined their names to create a name for one of the babies, and they were glad that one of the twins was named after the aunt they all loved so much. A few days later, Padre Arteta came to the house and baptized the babies "María Celia" and "Sara Teresa." Cecilia held Celia and Tía Sara held Sara as he sprinkled holy water over their heads. The babies didn't cry at all, but slept quietly throughout the ritual.

Celia slept in the crib that Papá had made for Sylvia, and Sara slept in a crib that Tío Santiago had hurriedly brought over from his house when it was discovered that Mamá had had twins. As Cecilia lay Celia in her crib, she said, "Fito and Belia are twins, but they're not identical. Celia and Sara look exactly alike. They really *are* identical. How can we tell them apart?"

Tía Sara went to her jewelry box and pulled out a tiny gold chain. She clasped it around Celia's arm. "There! Now we can tell them apart."

Everyone wanted to see the twins. Friends and family came from all the surrounding farms bringing plates of food, baskets of bread, and even cakes and pies. They knew how much work there is in a household with a new baby. And this household had two! Cecilia's friend Virginia and her mother came for a short visit. They brought a stew made with *carne seca*, meat that had been cut into strips and dried after the fall butchering.

"*¡Qué hermosas!* They are so beautiful!" Virginia said as she peered into the babies' cribs. "I'm so envious. I wish we had babies in our house." Virginia was an only child and often complained about being lonely. She envied Cecilia's house full of children, noise, and excitement.

"Well, you wouldn't envy me so much if you had to wash

their diapers," Cecilia complained. "Mamá can't get out of bed, and Tía Sara has too much to do in the house. I'm the one who has to wash their diapers. Look at my hands." Cecilia held out her hands for Virginia to inspect. They were chapped and cracked from wringing out the wet diapers in the cold afternoons. "I have to boil the diapers in a tub outside over a fire everyday after school. Then I have to rinse them in cold water, wring them out, and hang them on the line to dry. And this has been such a cold winter. Will it ever be spring?"

"I'll bring you my bottle of Jergens Lotion," Virginia offered. "You need it more than I do." Virginia suddenly felt lucky after all. Her parents were poor, so she wasn't pampered like Cecilia's cousins Belle and Clory. But since she was an only child, there was a lot less work in her home.

"Here, you can hold Celia. I'll hold Sara," Cecilia said. The two girls sat rocking the babies in their arms. Virginia sang:

> *"Duérmete niñita*
> *Que tengo que cocer*
> *Una camisita que te debes de poner*
> *En el día de San José."*

> "Sleep little baby
> For I have to sew
> A little shirt for you to wear
> On the day of San José."

WHEN THE TWINS were about six weeks old, Fito and Roberto came home from school with flushed faces and fever. They were coughing, sneezing, and had runny noses. Belia soon developed the same symptoms. By the next day, they were coughing and coughing, unable to breathe. Tía Sara thought they had a cold. She sent Elías to Tío Ben's store for a jar of Vicks ointment. She rubbed the strong-smelling ointment on their chests and covered them with a flannel cloth. Then she put them to bed and made them drink *té de yerba buena* with a little honey in it to soothe their coughing. The next day the children were feeling worse. Their eyes looked sunken in their heads and their mouths were dry. They coughed all day, and soon their coughs turned into loud whoops as they tried to get air into their lungs. Tía Sara feared they were ill with something much worse than a cold. With great apprehension, she checked on the babies in their cribs all day. They seemed to be fine.

Cecilia came home from school with terrifying news.

"The principal told us that there is an epidemic of whooping cough in the valley. He said it is very contagious, and we should all take precautions."

Whooping cough! Tía Sara had feared that this was what ailed the children. Before long, everyone, including the babies, was suffering from whooping cough, except for Papá and Cecilia. Mamá and the children lay in bed, hot and feverish, unable to breath or rest due to painful, uncontrollable coughing spells. Cecilia did what she could to make everyone comfortable. She went from room to room, slapping their backs as they choked during their coughing fits. There was no cure for whooping cough, so there was no point in sending for Dr. Steele in Hatch. Only time and rest would take care of them.

Cecilia became exhausted from trying to cook meals, tend to the sick, and look after Mamá and the babies. Mamá did what she could to feed the babies and change their diapers. Still, the twins were becoming undernourished. Papá bought cans of Eagle Brand Condensed Milk at Tío Ben's store to nourish the babies. It was the only milk that didn't need refrigeration. Papá took on the strenuous job of washing the babies' diapers over the outdoor fire. Mamá and Tía Sara were too ill to do any of their chores. They lay in bed, coughing and coughing, straining to get air into their lungs.

During this difficult time, Cecilia was unable to attend school. It was simply not possible. She and Papá were the only ones who weren't sick. While Cecilia tended to her brothers and sisters, she fretted about missing school. She knew there was no way now she could keep her A average. Her grade point would be ruined. It would be impossible to make up weeks of missed work. The idea of actually failing some of her classes filled her with horror. She had never made a failing grade in her life. Her greatest pride was her academic success. She studied hard and worked hard to learn her lessons and make good grades. She had struggled against Mamá to be able to attend high school and now all of this was in jeopardy. She might have to drop out of school altogether! She knew if she dropped out now, she would never go back to high school, and all her dreams would be unfulfilled. All these thoughts ran through her head over and over as she cleaned bed pans, changed diapers, carried pails of water, washed bed linens, and fed everyone bowls of hot broth. At night the thinking stopped as she stumbled into bed and fell asleep instantly from exhaustion.

Papá did as much as he could, but he had the farm and the animals to tend. Mamá saw her oldest daughter grow thinner. Her heart ached when she looked into Cecilia's hollow-eyed face. It pained her to see the exhaustion and lifelessness in Cecilia's eyes. Great love and pride for her daughter welled up in her chest. Why then was it so hard for her to tell her daughter she loved her?

After several weeks, it became apparent that everyone was getting better except for little Sara. The twin was losing weight and her skin was gray and dry, instead of the healthy pink color of Celia's skin. She coughed and cried all day and night, but no tears came from her eyes. She was too dehydrated. Mamá tried to give her water in a bottle, but the baby refused to drink. Cecilia saw the fear in Mamá's eyes. *Surely little Sara will get better,* Cecilia thought. *I just need to pray more for her.* Tía Sara was already saying a *novena* to Santa Teresita, Sara's patron saint. She would say the same prayer for nine days.

Cecilia knelt in front of her statue of Santa Cecilia, her patron saint. She was going to make a *manda*, a promise to the saint.

"Santa Cecilia, please make the baby well. Please don't let her die. I will say one hundred Hail Marys in your name if you intercede on her behalf." And so Cecilia began to pray. She knelt for hours on the hard, cold floor saying part of her *manda*. Surely Santa Cecilia would hear her prayers and keep the baby safe. All night Cecilia tossed and turned in her bed. She couldn't sleep for worrying about Sara. She could hear Mamá and Tía Sara praying in low tones in the next room as they rocked the baby and tried to give her water.

"Yo te bendigo desde la tierra, bendíceme tú desde el cielo. I bless you from earth, bless me from Heaven."

In the early hours of dawn, Cecilia thought she heard them crying.

Daylight on her face woke her. Cecilia jumped out of bed to go check on Mamá and the babies. The floor was cold under her bare feet. She found Mamá asleep in her bed. Her tired face looked as white as the sheet she lay on. Celia was nestled in the crook of her arm. Cecilia knew it was Celia because she wore the gold chain. Where was the other baby? Where was Sara?

Tía Sara tiptoed into the room and motioned for Cecilia to follow her into the warm kitchen. She hugged Cecilia to her chest and said, "Our little Sara did not live. *Es la voluntad de Dios. Está con los ángeles.* She is with the angels now." Cecilia sobbed as Tía Sara held her tightly. Her baby sister had died! Mamá and Papá had lost a child. Poor little Celia would have to grow up without her twin sister. How could such a terrible thing happen? How would they ever cope with so much sadness?

Elías made a tiny coffin out of wood, barely bigger than a shoebox. Papá, with red swollen eyes, went to the Iglesia de San Isidro to make funeral arrangements with Padre Arteta. At the church the bells in the tower had been tolling for days, signaling the death of someone from whooping cough. The poor priest was exhausted from going from farm to farm, giving the last rites to the dying and providing comfort to the living.

That night Papá, Mamá, Tía Sara, Elías, and Cecilia, together with family and friends who came to pay their respects, held a wake over Sara's little coffin. The younger children were put to bed. Tía Sara had sewed a tiny white dress for Sara and had placed a wreath of white silk flowers around the baby's head. During the *velorio* the women knelt around the coffin which sat on the parlor table surrounded with candles. They prayed the rosary and recited other *oraciones* all night. The men stood outside in the frigid air around a bonfire they had built, smoking cigarettes and drinking whiskey to stay warm. Inside the kitchen, some of the women fried donuts in lard and brewed strong coffee to help the others stay awake. During a break in the praying, Papá came inside and played his violin. He played with such feeling and with such sadness that people said, "He makes the violin cry. *Lo hace llorar.*"

The next afternoon, when the day had warmed a little,

Padre Arteta led the funeral procession down the road and up the hill to the cemetery. Papá and Elías had dug a small grave that morning in a dry, rocky spot near the graves of Mamá's family. Sara's coffin would be placed high above the fields next to the tall headstones marking the graves of Mamá's parents, Domenico Luchini, and his wife, Eusebia.

As the procession trudged up the rocky hill, Padre Arteta swung his incense burner, sending little puffs of smoke and a sweet aroma into the air. Papá carried Sara's coffin behind the priest, while Mamá and Tía Sara followed. Mamá walked with her back straight and her eyes dry. Always proud, she would never let anyone see her cry. Behind them came their children, family, friends, and neighbors. Mamá and Tía Sara were dressed completely in black, their heads covered with a black *chal*. Their shawls helped keep them warm in the brisk wind of the winter afternoon. In their hands they carried rosaries. When they reached the cemetery, Padre Arteta sprinkled holy water over the ground. The women began to sing.

> *"Bendito, bendito, bendito sea Dios,*
> *Los ángeles cantan y alaban a Dios,*
> *Los ángeles cantan y alaban a Dios.*
>
> *"O cielo y tierra, decid a una voz,*
> *Bendito por siempre, bendito sea Dios,*
> *Bendito por siempre, bendito sea Dios."*

"Blessed, blessed, blessed be the Lord,
The angels sing and praise the Lord,
The angels sing and praise the Lord.

"Oh, heaven and earth, say with one voice,
Blessed forever, blessed be the Lord,
Blessed forever, blessed be the Lord."

WILL SPRING ever come? Cecilia wondered for the hundredth time as she came home from school a few weeks after the funeral. Another heavy snow had fallen a few days ago, trapping everyone inside. The family had huddled in the warmth of the kitchen as they mourned the loss of the baby. *Was it my fault?* Cecilia wondered. *Did I complain too much about all the extra work, about having to wash diapers, about having to take over Mamá's duties? Was one baby taken from us to punish me?* She thought about the *manda* she had made to Santa Cecilia and about the many candles she had lit to San Judas in hopes that the baby would get well. Why hadn't her prayers been answered? Maybe she hadn't prayed hard enough. Maybe she hadn't prayed enough for *two* babies!

Once again Cecilia found comfort in the confessional at the Iglesia de San Isidro.

"Cecilia, we cannot presume to know God's reasons. Your little sister was not the only child to die from whooping cough," Padre Arteta said gently. *"Dios da y Dios quita.*

God lends us children, and sometimes he calls them back. He heard your prayers—never doubt that. Sometimes he answers our prayers in ways that we don't understand. He had a reason and a special place in heaven for Sara, but he left us Celia to love and to cherish."

When Cecilia got home from her confession, she found Belle waiting for her in her bedroom. Belle's pretty brown eyes were red and puffy. It was obvious she had been crying. She held a lacy handkerchief to her nose.

"Belle! What's wrong? *¿Qué te pasa?*" Cecilia asked.

"Oh, Cecilia, something terrible has happened! My life is ruined! Adrian has joined the Marines!" cried Belle as she threw herself across the bed. She sobbed into a pillow.

"What do you mean? How could he do that?" Cecilia asked in surprise. She was genuinely concerned for her cousin. She hated to see Belle so upset. She sat down on the bed next to Belle.

Belle sat up and through her sobs said, "A recruiter came to Hatch from El Paso. He convinced Adrian to enlist. We're not going to elope after all. Adrian says we'll have to wait until he finishes his tour of duty. But he'll be gone for at least two years!"

Cecilia smiled to herself. As usual, Padre Arteta was right!

CHAPTER 7

Cada cabeza es un mundo.

Every mind is a world.

On the first of March, smooth white snow covered the fields like frosting on a cake. But within a few days it had all melted. The afternoons were getting warmer, but the weather was still cold enough for Cecilia to enjoy wearing the brown wool suit she had made in home economics class. The suit had a straight mid-calf skirt with a matching belted jacket. Cecilia had never owned anything like it, and it made her feel stylish and modern. The suit was as beautiful as anything Loretta Peacock and the other town girls wore. And she had made it herself! Cecilia and Belia spent hours embroidering flowers in the corners of their homemade handkerchiefs, but Cecilia never realized she could actually sew such a well-tailored suit. With Tía Sara's and Miss Gustafson's help, Cecilia had discovered a talent she didn't know she possessed.

She was grateful for the warm suit when she got off the bus after school and walked the few yards home. The air was cold and breezy. The wind blew the clouds, making quick-moving shadows on the ground. In her arms she carried a heavy pile of schoolbooks. She had makeup work to do in every class. But her worst terrors had not materialized. The whooping cough epidemic had swept through the entire county, and the schoolrooms had been empty for weeks. Cecilia had not been the only one to miss weeks of school. Everyone was behind, and the teachers frantically tried to make up for lost time.

As Cecilia approached her house, she was startled to see Dr. Steele's car parked in front. He must have come all the way from Hatch. Fear gripped Cecilia. Who was sick now? She rushed into the kitchen.

"Hello, Cecilia. How are you feeling?" Doctor Steele asked. He was sitting at the kitchen table enjoying a cup of coffee with Papá and Mamá. Cecilia relaxed.

"I'm fine, thank you," she answered. She gave him a questioning look.

"I've been making some rounds, visiting your neighbors to make sure everyone has recovered from the whooping cough," Doctor Steele said. "I thought I'd drop in and check on things here. But your father says everyone is doing well."

Everyone *was* doing well except for Mamá. Although she had physically recovered from her pregnancy and the whooping cough, she suffered deeply the loss of her baby.

She didn't rise as early in the morning, she didn't move with her usual briskness and she rarely smiled. Cecilia noticed her eyes were often red against her pale face.

Cecilia refilled their cups with hot coffee and went to change her clothes. Then she picked up the pail of dirty diapers and went outside to begin the tedious job of washing them. Her parents and Tía Sara came out to walk Doctor Steele to his car. Fito, Roberto, and Belia had joined them on the porch.

"Hey! Get off my car, you old goat!" Doctor Steele shouted.

"¡Ay, Dios mío!" cried Mamá and Tía Sara at the same time. They were all horrified to see Roberto's goat Saltón on top of Doctor Steele's Model T Ford, chewing on the canvas roof. He stood calmly eyeing them as he swallowed a piece of canvas. Papá ran toward Saltón, yelling and waving his arms. The goat bit off another piece of canvas before jumping from the roof of the car. He ran through Mamá's garden, trampling the earth and disturbing some of her bulbs and seeds. Roberto ran right behind him.

"Well, would you look at that!" Doctor Steele said. "I heard goats will eat anything, but I can't say as I've ever seen anything like that before!" He broke into a loud guffaw. As he drove off, they could hear him laughing over the sound of the motor.

"¡Ay, qué vergüenza!" Mamá said. "I am so embarrassed. Roberto must have left Saltón's pen open. Where did that good-for-nothing boy go?"

Papá and the other children couldn't speak for laughing. Papá laughed so hard, tears came from his eyes. Even Tía Sara was laughing at the memory of the goat calmly standing on and chewing the roof of the car. But Mamá did not laugh.

"Ustedes no ayudan. Don't I have enough problems? This is not funny! We will have to offer to pay for the roof, and Roberto must be punished," Mamá said. And she went inside to look for the *chicote,* the leather strap that stung so hard when she whipped it against the children's legs. She came back out on the porch holding the whip, waiting for Roberto to return. She waited and waited. The others got bored and went off to do their chores. Finally, she grew tired of waiting and went inside to feed Celia and begin cooking supper. The afternoon darkened into evening as the family gathered around the table, but there was still no sign of Roberto. Mamá still had an angry gleam in her eye, but Cecilia was worried. She knew Roberto was afraid of a whipping and must be hiding somewhere. He would be cold and hungry. By bedtime, even Mamá was starting to worry.

"Vale más ir a buscarlo. Go look for him," she told Papá. He and Elías took kerosene lanterns and went out into the dark. They searched Saltón's pen first. The goat stood placidly munching some straw, but there was no sign of Roberto.

"Don't look so innocent, Saltón," said Elías. "You're the reason we're having to go to all this trouble. You're just lucky we don't turn you into *cabrito* and eat you for dinner!" Then he laughed and scratched the goat's head.

They checked the barn and the outhouse. They called Roberto's name in the darkness. Elías yodeled as he did when he called his brothers in from the fields, but there was no answer. Where could he have gone?

"Maybe he'll sneak back in during the night," Elías said. "Or maybe he'll hide under the hay in the barn—it will be warm enough there." Papá agreed. He knew Roberto would have to come back in his own time.

Early in the morning when the family was seated at the breakfast table, they heard footsteps and voices on the porch. Elías jumped up to open the door, and there stood Doña Carlota with her hand resting on Roberto's shoulder.

"¿No tienen un cafecito?" Doña Carlota asked as she shuffled into the warm kitchen. "A hot cup of coffee would be nice after our long walk." She sat down with a sigh in Elías' empty chair. Everyone stared in surprise. Fito's eyes were wide with shock. Roberto was with the *bruja!*

As soon as Mamá had gathered her wits, she said, *"Claro que sí.* Cecilia, pour Doña Carlota a cup of coffee." Everyone sat expectantly, wondering what would happen next. Roberto sat meek and silent in his chair. His hair needed combing, and his face and hands were grubby. Tía Sara shook her head at him, murmuring "tsk, tsk" under her breath. He looked down guiltily.

"¡Qué rico el café!" Doña Carlota said. "Perhaps I could have one of those *molletes* with a little butter. I didn't have time to fix myself breakfast this morning." Cecilia quickly

prepared a plate of food for the old woman. Doña Carlota began to eat with relish and downed another cup of coffee. She didn't say another word until she had wiped her plate clean with the last bite of bread.

Finally she spoke. "Your son stayed in my house last night. He seems to have gotten lost in the dark. He wanted to come home, but I heard an owl hooting outside my window. When an owl hoots, it is best to stay indoors," she said looking meaningfully at each of them. "Best to wait until the light of day to go out. Roberto was kind enough to escort me to your home. I have brought you some spices for your *caldo*," she added. Doña Carlota pulled out a small bag of dried herbs from her pocket and handed it to Mamá. "You'll like this seasoning. *Cominos, yerba buena, asafrán, and cilantro.* It makes a good soup."

Mamá thanked Doña Carlota for the spices and for looking after Roberto. While they waited for Papá to hitch the horses to the wagon to take Doña Carlota home, Mamá filled a bag with food for the old woman to take home. She knew her neighbor depended on the kindness and generosity of others for her survival. And although Mamá knew Doña Carlota was a *curandera* and not a witch, it was always better to be on the safe side of things.

When Roberto came home from school that afternoon, Mamá and Papá were waiting for him with the *chicote*.

"You must be punished for letting Saltón out of his pen and for running away. You made us all worry," she said angrily. *"José, castiga a tu hijo.* You must punish your son."

"Me va doler más a mí que a tí," Papá said. "This will hurt me more than you." His feet were dragging just as much as Roberto's as he took Roberto behind the barn. But what actually happened there, no one ever knew, because neither Papá nor Roberto ever said a word about it.

ONE COLD WINDY afternoon Cecilia came home from school feeling very hungry. She found baked sweet potatoes warming on the shelf above the stove. Mamá had left them there as an after-school snack for her children. Cecilia cradled a hot sweet potato in her cold hands and went in search of her mother and aunt. She found them in the back bedroom putting clean sheets and blankets on the two small guest beds. Cecilia noticed the room had been aired and a carpet placed on the floor. The furniture from the *jacal* had been moved into the large room.

"Are we having visitors?" asked Cecilia as she nibbled her hot potato.

"No, *hija.* A teacher and her grandmother will be renting this room from us. Her name is Georgia Dines. She's moving from Hillsboro to teach in Hatch, and they need a place to live. *Gracias a Dios.* Lord knows we need the money," Mamá said. Cecilia was excited. Imagine having a teacher in the house! *I'll have someone to help me with my homework and to talk about the books I'm reading*, she thought. *I hope she's nice.*

Georgia Dines *was* nice. She was a pretty young woman

with a bright smile and an energetic personality. She and her grandmother were grateful to have a place to stay and looked forward to getting to know the family. They would pay Mamá and Papá for the room, but they would cook their own meals on the small wood stove that sat in a corner. Fito and Roberto kept them supplied with chopped wood and kindling and pumped water for them every day. Georgia made the room warm and cozy by hanging colorful Indian blankets on the walls and placing a furry bearskin rug on the floor. She kept a fire going in the wood stove all day to keep her grandmother warm.

Georgia and Cecilia became instant friends. Georgia was a tiny woman with a big smile. She giggled with Cecilia like a schoolgirl. And best of all, Georgia had a typewriter which she allowed Cecilia to keep in her own room. She showed Cecilia the correct fingers to use on each key and even gave her paper to practice on. Cecilia's fingers flew over the black round buttons, causing the metal keys to strike the paper. She would fill up one side of the paper with typed lines, and then she would turn it over and type all over the backside. Paper was expensive and hard to get on the farm. She couldn't waste a bit of it.

Clack, clack, clack. Clickety clack. Cecilia would practice typing late into the night. Belia slept right through the noise, but many nights Mamá would wake up and come into the bedroom.

"*Ya basta con ese ruido.* Stop that racket and get to bed.

I can't sleep with all that noise. Why are you wasting your time with that machine?"

But Cecilia kept practicing every chance she got. Mamá might not understand, but Cecilia knew that if she were a good typist, she would be able to work in an office someday. This was Cecilia's dream—to live in a big city, work in an office, and earn her own money. She practiced for weeks, and soon she could type as well as Miss Dines. The teacher was so proud of Cecilia that when she moved back to Hillsboro the next year, she gave her the typewriter as a gift.

In February on Valentine's Day, Cecilia had brought home a thick stack of colorful valentines she had received from her friends at school. At least two of them were signed, *"Your Secret Admirer."* But Cecilia had wanted only one valentine— one from Johnny. Now she took the valentine he had given her last year from its hiding place behind a drawer in her dresser. Johnny had worked hard making a special, big red valentine in class. All the girls had wondered which girl would receive it on Valentine's Day. But Johnny hadn't given it to anyone—not until the last day of school in May when he shyly offered it to Cecilia. Now she held it tenderly in her hands and tried to keep her tears from spilling on it and spoiling the ink-written message, *"Will you be my valentine?"*

Throughout the Lenten season, the family did not eat meat on Fridays or during Holy Week. Mamá often fed the family on salted cod. The fish came dried and encrusted with salt in small wooden crates imprinted with the brand name

"Arbuckle." Cecilia had to soak the pieces of fish in a bowl of water to get the salt out. Mamá would add it to rice or use it to make fish soup.

Mamá also made *asadero* cheese during Lent. She put fresh cow's milk in shallow pans overnight. In the morning she skimmed off the cream that rose to the surface. The children raced to see who could get the cream first, but Mamá always made sure there was a dollop left for Papá's coffee. Mamá then added *trompillo* berries to the milk. During the summer, Fito and Roberto had picked wild *trompillo*, a plant with tiny yellow star-shaped flowers and little berries. Mamá picked off the berries and let them dry. The *trompillo* caused the milk to curdle into clumps. Mamá scooped up the clumps with her hands and squeezed out the water. She then put the clotted milk into a frying pan and stirred it continuously. The clumps turned into a stringy cheese that Mamá molded into thin patties. The children loved to eat *asadero* cheese on hot flour tortillas.

While Cecilia was helping Mamá in the kitchen, Elías, Fito, and Roberto were outside in the cold March air helping Papá with spring chores. The younger boys raked dead leaves and dried brush away from the corrals and orchards to prevent fires and to get rid of insects. Papá would burn the piles of leaves and brush later. Elías spent long afternoons repairing fences and helping Papá finish the plowing. Elías always took pride in the straight, even furrows he made with the horse-drawn plow.

Elías was learning from Papá how to handle problems on the farm. Yesterday Elías had watched as Papá treated a cow that had eaten bad alfalfa. The cow's belly had bloated up like a giant balloon, and the cow mooed in agony as it lay on the barn floor. Papá took his special sharp metal tool and poked a hole in the cow's belly, releasing the gas that had built up in her abdomen. The cow stood up in relief. Papá was often called on by the other farmers to perform this procedure on their sick cattle, as he was the only one in the valley who knew just how to do it without killing the cow.

CECILIA WAS EXCELLING in her first year of high school. It was everything she had imagined it would be. She had an unlimited source of books in the school library and even had a study period each day in which to read them. She had managed to keep an A average in every class and was hoping that she would be valedictorian when she graduated in three years. Maybe she could even win a scholarship to a college!

Cecilia no longer felt out of place among the other students in school. She had made many new friends among the town girls. But she especially liked Loretta Peacock, who ate her lunch with Cecilia and Virginia every day. Sometimes at lunch they would walk over to Busby's Drugstore and look at the displays of makeup and other cosmetics. Loretta often bought a new lipstick or a small bottle of cologne, allowing Cecilia and Virginia to sample them. Once, Cecilia had a quarter that Tía María had paid her for cleaning her house, and she bought five-cent vanilla ice cream cones for herself and her two friends. They sat at the soda fountain counter with other students who nonchalantly sipped Coca-Colas through straws, their legs dangling from the tall stools. She enjoyed listening to the modern way they spoke.

"Gee whiz! Did you see the snazzy tin can Eddie Brazeal was driving? It must have cost a lotta dough!"

"Aw, you're all wet. He got it second-hand in Las Cruces."

"Yowsah, that's what I heard."

"Well, Eddie's a good egg. He'll give us a ride in it."

"Hot diggity dawg!"

Soon Cecilia found herself saying things like "oodles," "all dolled up," and "it's just ducky."

Cecilia was still amazed at the freedom some of the other girls had compared to her. They rode in cars with boys and went on dates at night. She knew Mamá would never let her ride in a car with a boy. Mamá wouldn't even let her take P.E. in school because the girls had to suit out in shorts. Cecilia envied the other girls as she sat on the sidelines and watched them play basketball and volleyball in the gymnasium. Belle wore her shorts proudly although she didn't really enjoy all the physical activity.

"I don't like to sweat, but I like the way I look in shorts. I have such pretty legs," she said. Belle received her share of whistles from the boys. She was one of the prettiest girls in school. Cecilia knew Mamá would be horrified if a boy ever whistled at her.

Lost in her thoughts, Cecilia didn't hear her English teacher call her name. Another student poked her, and she realized that everyone in the class was looking expectantly at her.

"Class, I'd like to announce that Cecilia won the short story contest! 'Dick Rowel's Luck' took first place! Cecilia, come up and get this brand new five-dollar bill. We're all very proud of you!" Miss Johnson said.

Cecilia was stunned. *My story won first prize! I won five dollars! I won, I won!* she thought. She had never had so much money in her life. Papá and Mamá would be so proud of her!

When she got home, she rushed into the kitchen with her news. Tía Sara clasped her hands together.

"¡Santo Dios! I knew you could do it!" she said.

"I'm proud of you, *hija*," Papá said as he enveloped his daughter in a giant bear hug. "I know you worked very hard on your story. *¡Felicitaciones!"*

They all looked at Mamá and waited for her to say something.

"Well, make sure you use your money wisely," she said. *"Mejor se guarda lo que con trabajo se gana."* And with those few words, she left the kitchen to go check on the baby.

That night at the supper table, all the children made suggestions as to how Cecilia should spend her windfall.

"Are you going to buy some new dresses?" asked Belia.

"No, she's going to buy some books, aren't you?" said Roberto.

But Cecilia did neither. After spending a little money on candy for the whole family, she put her prize money away in the secret space in her dresser where she kept the valentine Johnny had made for her. She would need this money someday when all her dreams came true.

THAT YEAR a series of misfortunes struck the small town of Hatch. The train depot burned to the ground, the bank was robbed in broad daylight during the lunch hour, and a torrential rain flooded the town. Doña Carlota attributed it to witchcraft. But the citizens knew it was due to faulty wiring and a bank employee's failure to lock the door when he went home for lunch. As for the rain, well, as Tía Sara often said, *"En abril, aguas mil."* Everyone knew April brought rain.

On the day of the heaviest wind and rain, Tía Sara said, *"Cuando hace viento, quédate adentro."* Mamá kept the children inside. Belia entertained herself making paper dolls by cutting out figures from old catalogs. Papá repaired bridles and shoes, and Elías strummed his guitar, trying to learn a new song. The boys drove everyone crazy running through the house playing cowboys and Indians.

"May I look inside the family chest?" Cecilia asked Mamá. In Mamá's bedroom sat a beautiful old chest that had belonged to Mamá's father, Domenico Luchini. The chest was filled with important papers and family treasures Mamá wanted to protect. From time to time she would let the children entertain themselves by looking through the chest.

"¡Qué buena idea!" Tía Sara said. "I haven't looked inside the trunk in a long time." She and Cecilia sat on the floor while Mamá pulled out one treasure after another.

"Here is the baptismal outfit you wore as an infant, Cecilia. And here is the beautiful cap your tía made for you," Mamá said as she held up the delicate baby's cap edged with lace.

"You were such a beautiful baby," Mamá told Cecilia. "All my babies were beautiful," she said wistfully, and Cecilia knew Mamá was thinking of her little Sara, the child she had lost.

"Oh! Here is the little bank in the shape of a dog!" cried Cecilia. She had played with the heavy cast-iron bank when she was a child. She held it up now to divert her mother's attention from the baby's cap. "It still has some coins in it."

"Sara, look at this." Mamá held up a small, embroidered pincushion. "Do you remember when our mother made this? We were just little girls. How I treasure it!"

"Look! Here is my grandfather's diary!" cried Cecilia. She loved to read Domenico Luchini's record of his life on the farm dating all the way back to 1900. She struggled to read his scratchy penmanship, which grew harder to decipher as his age and increasing blindness caused him to scrawl illegibly. On April 3, 1903, he wrote:

"En este día tuvimos un fuerte viento que fue un verdadero huracán con una velocidad de 80 millas por hora y una lluvia torrencial."

"Imagine!" cried Cecilia. "Over 30 years ago, my grandfather was inside this very house sitting out a storm just as we are!"

Cecilia continued to read from the diary. She was fascinated by his comments on the major events of his day. On April 18, 1906, he wrote about the San Francisco earthquake. On March 24, 1909, he noted that ex-President Theodore Roosevelt was leaving for Africa to hunt wild game. At the end of the passage he had scrawled, "Good voyage, Colonel." He described how he had seen Halley's Comet in the western sky the evening of January 18, 1910. He wrote at length about the Mexican Revolution of 1910, criticizing the tyranny and despotism of President Porfirio Díaz, whom he had taken Mamá and Tía Sara to see in El Paso.

"Look! He even wrote about the sinking of the Titanic in 1912!" Cecilia said excitedly. She read aloud from the diary:

"Es un naufragio sin paralelo en la historia de la navegación a través del Océano Atlántico. The wreck of the Titanic is without parallel in the history of navigation in the Atlantic Ocean. He was right! I read about it in school," Cecilia added.

After supper, the storm continued to rage. Mamá placed pails and tubs around the house where the ceiling had begun to leak. Papá looked out the windows nervously. The cotton plants were barely sprouting, and he knew the rain and hail would destroy them. He and Elías had worked so hard plowing the soil, planting the seeds, and hoeing the weeds that sprouted up among the plants. Now in one day, a storm would destroy weeks of labor. Papá strummed Elías' guitar to give his nervous hands something to do. Soon the children sat on the floor around him, not just to listen to the music, but also to feel safer during the storm. The wind and the rain beating against the windowpanes had everyone on edge. Papá realized the children were frightened.

"Did you know I was born on a night just like this?" he asked them.

"Tell us about when you were born. Tell us! Tell us!" they all cried as they crowded closer to his chair. Mamá settled herself in the rocking chair to rock Celia to sleep, and Tía Sara sat mending clothes by the light of a kerosene lamp.

"My father, your grandfather Juan Neponuseno Gonzales, was a horse tamer, *un domador*. He and his brothers caught and tamed wild mustangs up north near Socorro. Ah, they were beautiful horses! Sorrels, bays, pintos, palominos, blacks and buckskins. Tough, stocky, with big heads and flowing manes. My father and uncles would catch them after the winter when they were weak. Then they would drive them down to El Paso and sell them, sometimes to the officers at Fort Bliss. They would go farther down to Ysleta and cross into Mexico, where they would buy cattle. Then they would drive the cattle all the way back up to Palomas, San Antonio, and Socorro, where they would sell them to ranchers and farmers. They had to ride through storms like this and fight off Apaches who tried to steal their cattle. Did you know my grandfather Eugenio was killed by Apaches?" Papá asked. The children had heard the story many times before, but they loved hearing it, and now they shook their heads, "No." Papá continued.

"He was shot by an Apache Indian in an argument over some cattle. He left his wife with eight children to raise. Your grandfather Juan was one of them. Juan married a beautiful woman named Petra Pagasa. They had five children before she died. Juan needed to find a mother for his children. The next time he passed through Ysleta, he met a widow named Carmen Durán Apodaca de Alderete. She herself had two children. She wasn't as beautiful as Petra, but she was attractive enough."

At this, Mamá frowned. "Your mother was a fine woman," she said sternly. "Looks are not the only reason to marry."

Papá laughed. "Well, she had enough looks to have nine more children! I was the fourth child they had together. Juan and Carmen had decided to settle down and try farming in Loma Parda, which is now Derry. They received a land grant of 160 acres under the Homestead Act. On their way from Socorro to Loma Parda, they were caught by a terrible storm. There was lightning and thunder. Rain and hail poured down. Their wagon was sticking in the mud, and my father was having trouble controlling the horses. To make matters worse, my mother began having labor pains. They managed to reach the farmhouse of a friend, Donaciano Montoya. He wasn't a relative, but my father always called him "Primo."

"Now this farmhouse wasn't even as good as our little *jacal* out back. It was just an adobe shack with a roof made of *latillas*, sticks and poles. Juan managed to get Carmen into the house. But the shelter was only slightly drier than outside. Rain poured through the roof and the floor was flooded. Juan and Donaciano lifted Carmen onto the wooden kitchen table and helped her give birth to me. They had to make a tent over us of cowhides to keep the rain off us. That is why weather like this doesn't scare me," Papá boasted. "I was born in it!"

"Tell us again the names of all their children," said Belia. The children loved to hear the long list of his brothers and sisters.

Papá squinted his eyes and pretended to think hard. "They were Santa Cruz, Juanita, Jesús, Eduardo, Luisa, Ramón, Socorro, Felipe, Eugenio, Petra, Donaciana, Delfina, Rómulo, Cruzita, Tomasita, and José—that's me."

"What happened to everybody?" Belia asked. Most of the family who lived around them came from Mamá's side.

"Some of them moved on to California and some to El Paso," Papá said. "And many died of influenza during the epidemic of 1918. But I survived, and that is why my children are strong and hardy and not afraid of storms," he told them. "You come from a long line of horse tamers, cattle drivers, and ranchers. Our family is as strong and hardy as the wild mustang. One little storm won't keep us down!" And he strummed the guitar with a flourish.

The boys cheered and the women clapped their hands.

"*A la cama, todos,*" ordered Mamá. "It is time for bed." She hustled the children off to the bedrooms. Cecilia remained reading by the light of the kerosene lamp.

"*Mañana sembramos de nuevo,*" Papá said as he strummed the guitar. "We will plant again tomorrow."

CHAPTER 8

Ya llegó por quién lloraba.
        The one you cried for has arrived.

P apá and the boys had been planting cotton, chile, alfalfa, and corn all spring. The pear, apple, peach, plum, and apricot trees in the orchard were starting to bud. Water was flowing in the canals and irrigation ditches. The ditch rider Tomás Gonzales, one of Papá's cousins, came by to check on the flow of water to Papá's fields. "Hey, boys, there's lots of perch in the canals. Maybe you can catch yourselves a few."

"Yippee!" they yelled as they ran to the large canal on the other side of the road.

"Why do *we* have to wash the diapers and do the laundry? We never get to go fishing," Belia complained. "I'd rather be fishing than boiling dirty baby diapers." She stood over a large cauldron and stirred the diapers with a wooden pole. Cecilia was rinsing diapers in a tub of cold water, wringing them out by hand, and hanging them on the clothesline with wooden clothespins she carried in a bag tied around her waist.

"Because Mamá says it's woman's work. I would rather be fishing, too." She sighed as she looked at the pile of dirty clothes they still needed to launder. She could think of a hundred things she would rather be doing on this beautiful spring morning. She had a new book she had checked out of the school library, and she could hardly wait to start reading it once all her morning chores were done. She gazed wistfully at her favorite reading spot under the tall cottonwood tree where lemon-colored sunlight fell on the soft ground. "Let's hurry and finish so you can go with the boys."

A half hour later, Belia sat on the bank of the canal and watched as Fito and Roberto stood in the waist-deep water, each holding one end of a large screen under the water. Each time they lifted the screen, there was a small fish or two wiggling in the center. They held up the screen for Belia to pluck the fish and put them in a bucket.

"We're catching supper for everyone," boasted Roberto.

"Don't be so sure," warned Belia. *"Del plato a la boca se cae la sopa."*

Belia longed to get in the canal herself, but she knew Mamá would be angry. Now that she was almost 12, she couldn't join her brothers in all their activities as she could when she was younger. *"Ya tienes que comportarte como una señorita.* You must behave like a young lady now." It seemed as if Mamá was telling her this more and more lately. Belia had been so used to running wild with her brothers that now these new constraints chafed her. *I wish I had been born a boy,* Belia thought.

When the air started to cool and the sunlight grew dimmer, Fito and Roberto counted over 20 perch in their bucket. Before going home, they wet their heads with canal water as Mamá had taught them to do. If the children got their feet wet, Mamá insisted that they wet their heads to avoid getting a cold. They ran proudly to the kitchen to show Mamá their catch. Small and bony, the fish were not very good for eating, but Mamá rolled them in flour and fried them in lard. Everyone ate a few at the supper table and proclaimed them delicious.

"There is a talent show at school next week," Cecilia told the family at supper. "Elías and I are going to perform. He is going to play the guitar, and I am going to sing. All the parents are invited," she added hopefully.

Papá raised his coffee mug to his lips. Mamá said, "We don't have time to go to the school. We have too much work to do here. We can hear you play and sing at home." Disappointment showed on Cecilia's face.

"I am sure you will perform beautifully," said Tía Sara. "What are you singing?"

Cecilia brightened. "We are going to sing *Cielito Lindo.*"

Cecilia and Elías did perform beautifully at the talent

show. They stood on the stage in the school gymnasium in front of a large audience of students, teachers, and parents. Elías and Cecilia had sung the words to the well-known song since they were children.

"Ese lunar que tienes, cielito lindo, junto a la boca
No se lo des a nadie, cielito lindo, que a mí me toca.
Ay ay ay ay, canta y no llores
Porque cantando se alegran, cielito lindo, los corazones."

"De la sierra morena, cielito lindo, vienen bajando
Un par de ojitos negros, cielito lindo, de contrabando.
Ay ay ay ay, canta y no llores
Porque cantando se alegran, cielito lindo, los corazones."

"That beauty mark you have, pretty little heaven,
    next to your mouth
Give it to no one, pretty little heaven, as it belongs
    to me.
Ay ay ay ay, sing and don't cry
Because singing, pretty little heaven, makes hearts
    happy."

"From the dark mountain, pretty little heaven, come
    descending
A pair of little dark eyes, pretty little heaven, of
    contraband.

Ay ay ay ay, sing and don't cry
Because singing, pretty little heaven, makes hearts
  happy."

AFTER ALL the enthusiastic applause, Elías and Cecilia were awarded the second-place ribbon. Even Elías, who never liked drawing attention to himself, was proud. *If only Mamá and Papá had been there to see us,* Cecilia thought as they rode the school bus home that night. She had scanned the audience while she and Elías were singing, hoping to see Papá and Mamá sitting in front of the stage after all. But she had been disappointed. She knew Papá was tired from working hard all day in the fields, and Mamá had to take care of the baby. She also knew Mamá mourned little Sara and wouldn't consider it seemly to attend any kind of festive gathering. But still, it would have made the evening perfect if Mamá and Papá had been there to see her and Elías win second place. Deep inside she felt as if Papá and Mamá didn't feel she was important enough for them to make the long trip to the school.

Perhaps Mamá was trying to make it up to Cecilia for missing the talent show, for to Cecilia's surprise, she gave Cecilia and Elías permission to go on a school field trip to White Sands National Monument. They would ride a school bus almost all the way to Alamogordo. Cecilia was excited. She had been to Alamogordo before to visit her cousin Carmela, but she had never been to White Sands. She could hardly wait to see one of the world's greatest natural wonders in the Tularosa Basin of New Mexico.

The school bus left early in the morning. After almost three hours, they arrived at the white sand dunes. The students ran up the dunes and rolled back down, not caring about their sand-encrusted arms and legs. It was like playing in a giant sandbox! The glare of the sun reflecting off the white gypsum sands was blinding. Cecilia was amazed. Looking at the miles and miles of glistening white sand dunes, she understood why the teachers had warned them not to wander off. It would be very easy to get lost. Cecilia, Virginia, and Loretta ate their lunches in the shade of one of the school buses.

"Where is Belle?" Cecilia asked. She hadn't seen her cousin since they had gotten off the bus.

"Oh, don't worry about her. I saw her walking behind that big sand dune with Felipe Tafoya," Virginia said. "He has a crush on her, and she's angry because Adrian hasn't written to her in weeks."

Cecilia thought about her cousin's brazen behavior. She was sure Belle and Felipe were kissing behind that dune. She knew what a big flirt her cousin was. With a start, Cecilia remembered Felipe was Johnny's cousin. She wondered if she herself would have walked behind a dune with Johnny if he had been there. Is that what Mamá was worried about all the time? That Cecilia might behave like some of the other girls? Is that why she never let Cecilia do anything or go anywhere? Cecilia trusted herself to make the right decision. How could she make Mamá learn to trust her?

Cecilia's head was filled with these questions as the bus made the long drive home. She hardly noticed the noise and the rowdy behavior of the boys on the bus. She was used to it by now. As the bus approached Hatch, the boys, tired from being pent up on the bus for hours, became rowdier, and a couple of them began to fight. The bus driver turned to yell angrily at them. Just at that moment, the bus approached a narrow curve, and the driver lost control. The bus made the turn too fast and fell over on its side! All the students lay piled on top of each other at the bottom of the bus!

Screams and shouts filled the air. The terrified students tried to untangle themselves as arms and legs flailed in every direction. A few of the boys managed to stand up and open the windows above them. They crawled out and pulled the others by their arms, helping them to climb out the windows. Finally, all of them were standing next to the overturned bus. Many of the girls were crying and everyone was brushing dirt and dust off their clothes. Miraculously, their injuries amounted to no more than scratches and bruises, although they would be sore the next day. The frantic teachers managed to calm everyone down. After checking that no one was seriously injured, the teachers told them they would all have to walk the rest of the way. The tired, sore and bedraggled group stumbled into Hatch thirty minutes later.

A different school bus drove the weary students to their

homes. Cecilia and Elías went into the kitchen with trepidation. What would Mamá say? Just as Cecilia had feared, Mamá became angry when she heard their story.

"*¿Qué negocios tenían ustedes en ese autobús?* What business did you have getting on that bus and going so far from home? I should never have allowed it!" Mamá said angrily. "Now go change your clothes. Look how dirty you are!" She continued to mumble to herself about dangerous bus trips and soiled clothing even after Cecilia and Elías had left the room.

"I don't understand why Mamá got so angry. It's not our fault the bus turned over," Cecilia said to Elías. Tears were making streaks down her dusty face. "She always blames everything on me!"

"Don't cry, *hermanita*," said Elías. "She will forget all about it tomorrow. Just don't stay up late reading tonight. You know how angry that makes her."

Cecilia did go to bed early that night. She was exhausted from the ordeal of the long bus ride, the bus turning over, and the walk to Hatch. It was just bad luck that the accident had happened. But now Mamá would feel justified in keeping Cecilia from participating in school functions. Cecilia plumped her pillow with her fist in frustration. Then she pulled the blanket over her shoulders and fell into a deep sleep.

CECILIA SAT in the rocking chair with Celia in her arms. The baby was wearing a bib Cecilia had made. On the front of the bib, she had sewn a little car that looked just like Dr. Steele's car. She had used scraps of fabric to appliqué the body and roof of the car onto the bib and had sewn on two tiny white buttons for the tires. Cecilia crooned to the baby as she rocked back and forth in the old rocker on the porch. The afternoon was warm enough to sit outside with the baby in the fresh air.

Cecilia had something on her mind. Her freshman class was going on a picnic to the Black Range on Saturday. Once again the students would be transported by a school bus. Belle was going. So was Virginia, Nestora, Loretta, Albert Castle, Al Hatch, and all of Cecilia's other friends. She desperately wanted to go, but she was afraid to ask Mamá for permission. She knew Mamá would say no after the bus accident. This time it wouldn't matter if Elías went or not. Mamá didn't want her children riding the school bus on a long trip. Cecilia thought about the fun all the others would be having, while she would be left out. She steeled herself to approach Mamá with her request.

"*¡No, señorita! Ni lo mande Dios.* Absolutely not!" Mamá said. "You are getting to be just like the town girls, always wanting to be going places when you should be home like a proper young lady. You will stay home where you belong and where you will be safe."

"But, Mamá, everyone is going. Belle will be there. I'll stay with her the whole time," Cecilia pleaded.

"No! And do not argue with me," Mamá said.

"Mamá, you are not being fair. Why can't I go? Why? Give me one good reason!" Cecilia said, her voice growing louder.

"I don't need to give you a reason. I am your mother. You will respect and obey me," Mamá said angrily.

"Why do you treat me like this?" Cecilia cried. "You let Elías do whatever he wants. You let the boys run wild all over. You won't let me do anything! I never do anything wrong! Why won't you trust me?"

"It is not a matter of trust. I know what is best for you. I do not want people thinking bad things about you. People will say I didn't raise my daughter properly. I do not want to be ashamed of my daughter," Mamá said angrily.

"You see?" Cecilia said. "It is not *me* you are thinking of. It is yourself!" She raised her voice louder. "You don't love me! You love all the others, but not me! I can't wait till I grow up and can leave here!"

Mamá reached out her hand and slapped Cecilia across her face. Cecilia was stunned! Mamá had never slapped her face before. Mamá had whipped her legs with the *chicote* when Cecilia was a child, but Cecilia was almost an adult now. She felt shamed and humiliated. She ran out the door and didn't stop running until she reached the barn. She went inside and fell on a mound of dried hay. She began to cry.

"*¿Qué te pasa, hija? ¿Porqué lloras?*" Cecilia felt Papá's hand on her head. "Why are you crying?" He knelt down beside her in the hay and took her in his arms. Cecilia rested her head on his shoulder.

"Mamá doesn't understand me! She doesn't love me!" Cecilia cried.

"No, Cecilia, that is not true," Papá said. "Your mother loves you very much. It is because she loves you that she tries to protect you. Your mamá is from another time. She sees things differently from you. Things are changing in the world. But it is hard for people to change. It is hard for parents to see their children grow up."

"But why won't Mamá trust me? Why won't she let me do what the others do?" Cecilia said.

"She does trust you. It is other people she does not trust. She only wants to keep you safe," said Papá. "It is a great responsibility being a mother. You will find that out someday for yourself. Right now you need to respect your mother's wisdom and experience." Cecilia had stopped crying and was listening to Papá's words.

"Do not be in a hurry to grow up. You do not have to do everything at once. Your mamá will learn to accept change little by little, just as you will learn to grow up little by little. Go to your mother now and be a good daughter to her. She loves you very much—just as I do," Papá said tenderly. His mustache pricked her skin as he kissed her on the cheek. He took a bandana from his shirt pocket and wiped the tears from her face.

Cecilia walked back to the kitchen. Mamá was standing at the hot stove, stirring a pot of beans. She looked tired and pale, and her eyes were red as if she had been crying. Cecilia felt a great tenderness for her mother, and she ran to her, burying her face in her chest. Poor Mamá had had to deal with her baby dying, and all Cecilia had done was cause her more problems by wanting to go to dances and picnics and other silly places. She had been so self-centered, thinking only of her dreams and her goals for the future and not of Mamá's grief.

"*Lo siento, Mamá.* I'm sorry, I'm sorry!" she cried.

Mamá held her close and stroked Cecilia's short brown hair. "I miss your braids," she said. "But you do look pretty this way."

Cecilia felt so flattered. Mamá never praised her like this. She threw her arms around her mother's neck and began to cry.

"I'm sorry, Mamá. Please forgive me. *Perdóname.* I have been a bad daughter to you. I have been disrespectful and disobedient. You work so hard for all of us. I need to help you more." Cecilia came to a sudden decision.

She pulled away from her mother and said, "I am going to drop out of school. I have been selfish, thinking only of myself. You need me here to help you. I won't go back to school," she said.

Mamá looked at Cecilia for a long time. Then she reached out her arms and pulled Cecilia to her chest. At last she spoke.

"No, *hija*, you must stay in school. It is what makes you happy. There has been enough unhappiness in this house." Mamá kissed Cecilia on her forehead, and Cecilia heard her murmur, "*Hija de mi corazón,* child of my heart."

"*Ándale, mija, ayúdame con la cena.* Help me get supper

ready," Mamá said with her usual briskness as she turned back to the stove. Cecilia, a large smile spreading across her face, began to set the table, and no more was said about the picnic.

A FEW DAYS LATER Tía Sara came to Cecilia's room. "Cecilia, your Tío Ben is going to El Paso on business. I have decided to go with him to visit my *comadre*, Señora Tafoya. Her mother has been ill a very long time. Would you like to go with me? Your mamá has given her permission."

Cecilia jumped up from her bed and threw her arms around her aunt's neck.

"*¡Ay, Tía!* Of course, I want to go!" she cried. She could hardly believe her ears! Tía Sara was taking her to El Paso to visit Johnny's mother. She would get to see Johnny!

"Belle will be going with us as well," added Tía Sara. "You girls will have a good time together and can keep each other company on the road. You always seem to have so much to talk about."

Cecilia was excited to be going to such a big city as El Paso. She had only been there once before to visit relatives. Her heart pounded with excitement. She went to Mamá to thank her for letting her go.

"Your tía is going with you. She will be a proper chaperone for you and Belle. Just be sure the two of you behave yourselves and do not give your uncle and aunt any cause for worry," Mamá said.

Cecilia refrained from reminding Mamá that she never

gave anyone cause for worry. She didn't want to do anything to jeopardize her trip to the city.

Early Saturday morning, Tío Ben piled them all in his car and began the long drive to El Paso. Tía Sara sat in the front next to her brother, while Belle and Cecilia chattered in the back.

"I'm sure we'll get to see Johnny," Belle said slyly as she gave her cousin a knowing look. "Won't that be swell?"

Cecilia refused to rise to the bait. "Of course. We haven't seen him in a long time, and everyone misses him at school. It will be fun to come back and tell everybody how he is doing in El Paso. Oh! Look at those huge nests in that tree!" she said in an attempt to change the subject. But she felt butterflies in her stomach at the thought of seeing Johnny again. *I hope he's glad to see me,* she thought.

"Those are mesquite trees, and the nests belong to hawks. Look! There is one now!" Tío Ben said. They all craned their necks to look out the windows at a hawk circling gracefully above them. Cecilia could see dust devils whirling in the distance, yet dark gray clouds were spilling rain on the mountains to the west.

They stopped for a picnic lunch at the ruins of Fort Selden. Tía Sara spread a tablecloth under a shady cottonwood tree and set out the meal Mamá had packed for them. After they had eaten, Tía Sara rested while Tío Ben walked with the girls around the ruins. Nothing was left of the fort except for the adobe walls of old buildings. Anything of value had long since been hauled off for other uses. The mud walls looked as if they were melting in the sun. Mount Robledo loomed over the fort, while the Rio Grande ran to the south.

"Try to imagine what the fort was like in the late 1800s," said Tío Ben. "These walls are all that are left of the stables, barracks, officers' quarters, and other buildings. We're standing in the middle of the parade ground. Notice how hard and packed the ground is. Hundreds of soldiers marched here over the years."

Cecilia thought of the soldiers marching proudly in their blue wool uniforms and carrying rifles. She could almost hear the drums beating, the trumpets blowing, the horses whinnying, and the officers shouting orders. She wondered if any of their ghosts lingered at the old fort, and even though the day was warm, Cecilia shivered. She ran back to Tía Sara.

"Look at all the cactus," Tío Ben told the girls. "This is Spanish dagger. That one is prickly pear. And that vicious-looking one is cholla. Don't ever touch that!" he warned. All about them grew salt bush, gray and tangled, along with creosote plants and a few mesquite trees.

As they headed toward the small town of Las Cruces, Tío Ben pointed out that they were following the Camino Real, the route early settlers used from Mexico City to Santa Fe. Conquistadors, missionaries, settlers, and traders had all passed this way.

"Over that way is the *Jornada Del Muerto*," Tío Ben said.

Cecilia had read about the dreaded "Journey of the Dead Man." Cecilia wondered what it was like to cross the desert without food or water and was glad *she* was traveling in an automobile on a paved road.

Cecilia caught her breath at the sight of the Organ Mountains. Tall, craggy peaks glistened silvery-white in the distance. She imagined that was what the surface of the moon looked like.

As they entered the bustling city of El Paso, Cecilia began to feel more and more excited. How different this was from home! So many streets—and they were all paved! So many houses and automobiles and people! *People are so lucky to live here*, Cecilia thought. *Someday I will, too.*

Tío Ben found Missouri Street near the downtown area and pulled up in front of a white house with green trim. They climbed up the steps to the wide front porch and rang the bell. Cecilia tried to brush the wrinkles out of her skirt. She fluffed up her hair with her fingers.

"Pasen, Pasen. ¡Bienvenidos!" said Señora Tafoya as she ushered them into a small, neat parlor where they were greeted by her daughter Cleofas. They sat down and Cleofas served them coffee, lemonade, and cookies. Cecilia looked about her expectantly. The front door opened and Johnny walked into the room. Cecilia's heart skipped a beat. He looked so handsome!

As was proper, Johnny greeted the adults first. Then he turned to Belle and Cecilia. Nervous and shy, Cecilia smiled up at Johnny. She felt her cheeks blushing as he smiled back at her. His smile grew wider and wider. Was that smile just for her?

"Hi!" he said. "How are things back home?" He sat down between the girls, and it seemed as if they all began to speak at once. They laughed and drank their lemonade and shared stories of their classes, their teachers, and their new friends. Cecilia wondered if Johnny would find a way to speak to her alone, to explain to her why he hadn't written as he had promised.

"I've really missed everyone back home," Johnny said, looking straight at Cecilia as he spoke. The butterflies in her stomach flapped their wings. "Both of you cut your hair," he told Cecilia and Belle. "It looks nice. I like it!"

Suddenly, the doorbell rang. Señora Tafoya rose to answer it.

"It is probably my neighbor. He used to live in Derry, and I told him you were coming to visit. He said he would like to see you," she said as she opened the door.

A tall, handsome man in a dark suit stood on the porch. He held his hat in his hands.

"Pase, pase," said Señora Tafoya. *"Les presento Edmundo Lucero."*

Tío Ben stood up to greet the visitor. But Tía Sara sat on her chair, as if rooted to the spot. Cecilia saw her aunt's face turn completely white and her eyes open wide with surprise. She looked as if she had seen a ghost!

"Ya conozco al Señor Lucero," Tía Sara said. "We have met before."

Suddenly, it made sense to Cecilia. Edmundo Lucero! That was the name of the man who had asked Tía Sara to marry him many years ago. Her father had refused his permission. He didn't feel Edmundo was good enough for his daughter. Cecilia had overheard Mamá and Tía Sara talking about it one night when they thought she was asleep. This must be the same man! No wonder Tía started to blush, and her face filled with color. Tía Sara stood up and offered her hand to Edmundo.

CHAPTER 9

Amor, salud, y pesetas, y tiempo para gozarlas.
Love, health, and wealth, and time to enjoy them.

Cecilia was right. The man *was* Edmundo Lucero who had been in love with Tía Sara when they were young. He had proposed marriage to her, but she had obeyed her father and had refused his proposal. Edmundo had left Derry soon after to heal his broken heart in a new place where there would be no memories of Sara. Tía Sara had always believed he had gone to California. She was shocked to learn he had settled as near as El Paso where he had his own small construction company.

Tío Ben thought the whole situation was funny and kept saying, *"¡Qué milagro!* What a miracle!" over and over until Tía Sara made him stop with an angry glance in his direction. Cecilia could tell her aunt was nervous and embarrassed to be suddenly face to face with her old love. Cecilia felt shy and nervous herself to see Johnny again. She was glad Belle was there to distract everyone with her chatter and high spirits.

"I'm tired of being in the car all day. Can't we go for a walk? I would love to see the alligators in the *placita*," Belle said. "And I'd love to show off my new dress."

"*¡Qué buena idea!*" said Johnny. "What a good idea! We can walk Downtown, and you can see San Jacinto Plaza. Just wait till you see the alligators!"

Cecilia had always wanted to see the alligators everyone talked about. They lived in a concrete pool of water in the middle of the plaza in downtown El Paso. People could lean against the concrete balustrade around the pool and watch the alligators glide in the water or sun themselves on the ground. Cecilia had never seen a real alligator in her life, although she had read about them in books.

While Tío Ben went off to settle his business, Cecilia, Belle, Johnny, and Cleofas walked to the plaza. Edmundo and Tía Sara followed a short way behind, lost in conversation. Señora Tafoya stayed behind to prepare a supper for their return. She promised them *un rico guisado*, a delicious stew. She would serve it with the green chile salsa and homemade flour tortillas Mamá had sent.

As they walked, Cecilia once again marveled at the sight of so many houses, people, and automobiles. It took her a while to get used to the noise of the cars as they whizzed by. As they approached the plaza, she was surprised by the sight of a strange-looking bus attached to wires that ran overhead.

"What is that?" she asked Johnny.

"That's the *tranvía*—the streetcar. I ride it all the time," he answered, proud to show off his knowledge of the city. "Well, here we are in downtown El Paso. Isn't it swell!" he said.

Cecilia and Belle looked in awe at all the tall buildings that encircled the plaza. Elegant hotels, department stores, restaurants, and enormous bank buildings many stories high filled the downtown area. It was so different from the small, quiet farming community where she had lived all her life. *How exciting to live in a place like this,* Cecilia thought. *All this noise, all these busy people rushing all over, all these modern buildings! I can't wait until I'm old enough to live here!*

Tía Sara and Edmundo sat on a park bench still absorbed in their conversation. Cecilia noticed that her aunt was laughing like a schoolgirl at something Edmundo had said to her. Cecilia had never seen Tía Sara look so young and happy. Her beautiful face lit up as she smiled at Edmundo. He took Tía Sara's hand in his and she blushed a deep red. *Can it be that Tía Sara is still in love with him?* Cecilia thought.

"I'm going to walk around the *placita*," said Belle after they had seen the alligators. "I want to see everything." She gave Cecilia a wink as she linked arms with Cleofas and took her to admire the trees and flowers in the plaza, something Cecilia knew Belle had no interest in whatsoever.

"Let's sit here," Johnny said. They sat on a park bench near the alligator pool. "I've been wanting to talk to you alone all afternoon. I'm sorry I haven't written you," he told

Cecilia. "I'm not very good at writing letters. I never know what to say. I hope you're not angry at me."

"Oh, I'm not angry!" Cecilia said. "I'm sure you've been very busy. There is so much to do here in the city," she said.

"Well, I know I should have written to you," Johnny said. "I promised I would. And I really wanted to get letters from you. But I was also afraid your mamá would get angry. Your Tía María runs the post office in her store and handles all the mail. Everyone knows she reads the postcards and checks all the return addresses on the envelopes. She knows everything that goes on in Derry. I was afraid she would tell your mamá I was writing to you. I didn't want to cause problems for you."

"I think if you would like to write me, it would be all right. I'd like to get a letter from you," Cecilia answered shyly. She felt her heart would explode—it was pounding so hard in her chest. Johnny took her hand and held it tightly.

"Would you? Then I'll write you a letter as soon as you leave!" Johnny said, and they both laughed. Cecilia felt enormous relief. Johnny didn't have a girlfriend. He still cared for her! Jeannie Vetter was right. Boys just don't like to write letters. She felt as if a large weight had been lifted from her chest. She felt happy and lighthearted for the first time in months.

"Cecilia, I've been wanting to tell you something for a long time," Johnny said, still holding her hand. "I think you're wonderful. I think about you all the time."

"Oh, Johnny, I feel the same way!" Cecilia admitted to

him. "I think about you so much I can't sleep at night!"

"Me, too!" he cried. "Let's stay awake and think of each other," he said. They both laughed.

"I'm so glad you came to visit. I've missed you a lot!" he said. Then Johnny did what Cecilia had been dreaming of all winter long—he leaned over and kissed her on the lips.

AS TÍO BEN drove them all back to Derry late that night, Cecilia thought about her wonderful trip to the city and the day's events. The alligators with their big jaws and sharp teeth had been an exciting sight she would never forget. Tía Sara had met an old sweetheart. But, of course, the best part was seeing Johnny again and finding out he still cared for her. She felt warm all over when she remembered Johnny's lips on hers, and she smiled to herself in the darkness. She was bursting with happiness and wished she could tell Belle all about Johnny and how she felt about him, but she knew Belle could never keep a secret. Besides, Belle had fallen asleep in the car.

In the front seat, Tío Ben concentrated on the road, while Tía Sara sat strangely quiet. Cecilia wondered, *Could Tía Sara be thinking about Edmundo? Does she love him the way I love Johnny?*

Cecilia and Tía Sara climbed into their beds after midnight, exhausted from the trip. Mamá allowed Cecilia to sleep late Sunday morning and miss mass with the family at the Iglesia de San Isidro. However, she made sure Cecilia knelt and prayed a rosary in front of the statue of the Virgin Mary as soon as she woke up and before she ate her breakfast.

All day Cecilia noticed that Tía Sara was unusually quiet, just like she had been in the car on the way home. Cecilia had done most of the talking when telling the family all the details of the trip. Belia wanted to know about her friend Cleofas, and Fito and Roberto couldn't hear enough about the alligators. They pestered Cecilia all day with questions. In the evening, Tía Sara came to Cecilia's room.

"*Quiero hablar contigo, sobrina.* I need to talk to you," Tía Sara said. Cecilia looked up from her book.

"*Sí, Tía.* Is something wrong?" she asked. Tía Sara seemed nervous, yet excited in a way.

"I need to talk to you about Edmundo. I wanted you to be the first to know," she said. "Yesterday Edmundo asked me to marry him." Tía Sara sat down on the bed and told Cecilia the story of Edmundo's first proposal many years ago and her father's rejection of their engagement. Her father didn't feel Edmundo would make a suitable husband for her. Edmundo's family had not been as well off financially as Sara's.

"I know I should have been stronger and fought my father for the right to marry the man I loved. But I had been raised to respect my father and obey his orders. Edmundo didn't understand. He believed I never really loved him, and he went away," Tía Sara said.

"Did you really love him?" Cecilia asked.

"Very much, and I have never forgotten him. Yesterday

192

he told me he has never forgotten me. He has never married, just as I have never married. He told me he still loves me and would like us to be married as soon as possible. If I agree, I will move to El Paso. Cecilia, what should I do?"

"Tía, do you want to marry him?" Cecilia asked.

"Yes. Yes, I do," Tía Sara said.

"Then what is holding you back this time?" Cecilia asked.

"How can I leave you and everyone else here? I love all of you so much. And your mother depends on me for help in running the house. I wouldn't feel right abandoning everyone!" Tía Sara said.

"Tía, you would not be abandoning us!" cried Cecilia. "You would be following your heart, your dream. You have told me over and over again that I should never give up my dreams. You have sacrificed enough for us. Now you must live for yourself!"

Tía Sara began to weep into her handkerchief.

"Tía, don't cry. You looked so happy with Edmundo. I'm sure that if my *abuelo* were alive today he would change his mind. Remember what he wrote in his diary when he was an old man?" Cecilia had memorized his words because they had made her feel he would approve of her dream to get an education and move to the city. She recited:

"Cuando un hombre o una familia se ve abatida en un lugar y que ve que la fortuna lo persigue en su contra, entonces es el tiempo de cambiar de clima. Dios formó los cuatro vientos para que el hombre los aproveche, y cambia la

corriente de la fortuna con cambiar de pueblo o estado."

"Tía, *abuelito* wrote that the four winds blow so we can follow them and change our lives, so we can take advantage of better places and better fortune somewhere else. It is what *he* did when he left his home in Italy and came all the way to Derry," Cecilia reminded her aunt. "Mamá would never want you to be unhappy. None of us would. We all love you too much." She hugged her aunt and kissed her cheek. "Besides, El Paso isn't so far away!"

"Thank you, Cecilia," Tía Sara said as she wiped her eyes. "You are right. I *do* need to follow my dream. I will go tell your mother and father that I am going to marry Edmundo! And tomorrow I will call Edmundo from Tío Ben's telephone and tell him I accept his proposal!"

ON THE FOLLOWING SUNDAY, Edmundo Lucero sat with Papá, Mamá, and Tía Sara in the parlor. He had come to make the *petición de mano*, the formal request for Tía Sara's hand in marriage. Edmundo looked very handsome in a dark suit and tie. He had a mustache, although it wasn't as big and black as Papá's. He sat smiling at Tía Sara and drinking Mamá's coffee. Tía Sara wore her best dress, and her mother's garnet earrings dangled from her ears.

Since Tía Sara's father was dead, Edmundo presented Papá with a formal letter in which he made his *petición*. Papá hated formality and now he said to Edmundo, "You read it, you read it."

Edmundo's hands trembled nervously as he took his letter from the envelope and read aloud:

"*Estimado Señor Gonzales, yo deseo entrar en matrimonio con su cuñada Sara Luchini.* I would like to marry your sister-in-law. I promise that I will love and honor her the rest of our lives. I will come back next week for your answer."

"No, no!" Papá said, once again dispensing with all tradition and formality. "If you two are agreed, you have my blessing right now!"

"Then we will go immediately to speak to Padre Arteta at the Iglesia de San Isidro and arrange for the bans to be read," Edmundo said, excitement obvious in his voice. Smiling broadly, he took Sara by the hand and whisked her off to the church in his car.

IN THE NEXT FEW WEEKS, the house was turned upside down. Everyone was absorbed in planning Tía Sara's wedding to Edmundo. Mamá took out her own bridal dress from her chest so that Tía Sara could alter it for herself. The dress was made of ivory silk and adorned with delicate lace and satin roses. Tía Sara would wear an ivory-colored lace *mantilla* on her head. Tía Sara was also busy sewing a new dress for Cecilia, who would be her *madrina* and her only attendant. Edmundo had brought beautiful satin fabric from El Paso for Tía Sara, and she had chosen to use it for Cecilia's dress. The leftover satin would be made into small pillows for the bride and groom to kneel on during the long wedding ceremony.

While Tía Sara was busy sewing on the old foot-pedal machine, Mamá was planning the wedding feast. Whenever wedding bans were read at church, everyone in the community knew they were all invited to the reception after the wedding mass. Mamá and Cecilia baked dozens of *bizcochitos*, the traditional wedding cookie. They mixed lard, sugar, flour, eggs, and crushed anise seed, which gave the cookies their special flavor. Cecilia rolled the dough on the kitchen table and cut it into small diamond shapes. After the cookies were baked, Cecilia dredged them in a mixture of sugar and cinnamon. She sealed them tightly in tin cans to keep them fresh until the wedding day. Cecilia was relieved to see Mamá acting like her old self again, moving about the kitchen briskly and efficiently.

Papá and the boys cleared weeds and brush from around the house and the garden. Elías gave the wood trim of the porch a new coat of green paint. Belia swept the long porch and helped Cecilia clean the house. They dusted and polished the furniture in the *sala* until it shone. Every time they finished one chore, Mamá had another one for them to do. But everyone was happy to work hard because they loved Tía Sara and wanted her to have a beautiful wedding day.

"Cecilia, you have a letter! It came in today's mail!" cried Belia from the kitchen door one day when Cecilia came home from school.

A letter! *It must be from Johnny!* Cecilia thought. He had said he would write. Belia handed her the envelope, and

Cecilia looked quickly at the return address. It wasn't from Johnny. It was from her friend Jeannie! Jeannie had written her all the way from California! Cecilia tore open the envelope in her excitement.

"What does she say? What does she say?" asked Belia. Cecilia read the letter aloud.

> Dearest Cecilia,
>
> I am sorry I did not write you sooner. But we have been very busy getting settled here in California. It's warm and sunny here. I saw palm trees for the first time. You would love to see them yourself. I know how you like to see new things.
>
> Pa got a job fixing cars. The boys and me are in school again. I am learning like you. I can read so much better now. I wore the dress you gave me to a school dance and it was as pretty as any dress there.
>
> We made the trip all right. But I am sorry to tell you Grammaw died right after we got here. Her heart just gave out. I think she was just wore out from the long trip and she missed our home in Oklahoma. We all miss our dog Jeep and hope he is doing fine.
>
> We all miss your ma's cooking. She sure is a good cook. The boys want me to say hey to Fito and Roberto. By the way, have you heard from you-know-who?
>
> Well I have to go now. I hope you will write me and tell me everything you are doing.
>
> Your friend forever,
> Jeannie Vetter

Cecilia read the letter over and over again. She hadn't realized just how much she missed her friend. She was glad that Jeannie and her family seemed to be happy in their new home. She would answer the letter right away and tell Jeannie about her trip to El Paso and Tía Sara's wedding. Jeannie would enjoy hearing all about her visit with Johnny—and his kiss! She put Jeannie's letter away along with Miss Malone's postcard. Now she had *two* pieces of mail all her own. If only *Johnny* would send her a letter! Jeannie had been right—boys just weren't very good at writing letters.

Cecilia had another piece of news to tell Jeannie in her letter. Class elections had been held, and Cecilia had been elected sophomore class secretary for the next school year. She felt honored to be chosen by her fellow classmates, and she would do her best to be a good class secretary.

Cecilia thought back to her first week in high school and laughed at herself. How could she have been so unhappy and unsure of herself? She had made many new friends and learned all kinds of new things. She had even learned to type, thanks to Miss Dines. Soon she would learn enough to be able to get a job in the city. Everything seemed to be going so well right now. After the baby died, Cecilia had wondered if the family would ever be happy again. Cecilia thought, *This must be what Tía Sara means when she says "Días de más, días de menos." Life is filled with good days and bad days. We have to accept both if we want to live fully.*

Cecilia thought about Tía Sara and her wisdom. How many

times had she comforted and counseled Cecilia through all her problems? She was the only person who seemed to understand Cecilia's dreams and goals for the future. She had always been there for Cecilia, sharing her secrets, encouraging her, giving her advice. What would Cecilia do without her? In all the excitement of the wedding preparations, Cecilia hadn't stopped to think just what life would be like without Tía Sara. Tears came to Cecilia's eyes. She would miss her aunt deeply, but she wanted her to be happy. She wouldn't let Tía Sara see her cry. She went now to find her aunt and wish her well in her new life.

Tía Sara was in the kitchen pressing her wedding dress with an iron she had heated on the stove.

"Cecilia, I am glad you are here. I need to talk to you. When Edmundo came to visit last Sunday, I spoke to him about you, and I told him how much I'm going to miss you. Cecilia, we would like you to come live with us in El Paso after we are settled. You could come in September and go to high school there," Tía Sara told her. Cecilia didn't know what to say. She was completely surprised and confused. She stood staring at her aunt, unable to speak. Tía Sara laughed.

"You do not have to decide right now. You have several months to think about it. But I want you to know that Edmundo wants this as much as I do," her aunt said.

Cecilia went outside to sit in the sun. Her head was spinning. So much was happening around her, she didn't know what to think. Tía Sara and Edmundo wanted her to live with them! She would be able to go to a big city high school. Why, she would go to the same high school as Johnny! She would get to see Johnny every day. She would be able to go to school functions, and she wouldn't have as many chores to do. She would have much more time to read and to spend on her studies. Mamá didn't appreciate her, anyway. As far as Mamá was concerned, Cecilia could never do anything right. Going to live in El Paso would be a dream come true! It would be everything she ever wanted!

Cecilia went back into the kitchen.

"Tía, have you talked to Mamá about my going to live with you?" Cecilia asked.

"*Sí, querida.* I have. Your mother said it would have to be your decision," her aunt answered.

Cecilia was stunned. She could hardly believe Tía Sara's words. Mamá was leaving it up to her to decide whether she stayed on the farm or went to live in the city with her aunt. Cecilia had felt for a long time that Mamá didn't respect her dreams, that Mamá didn't have faith in her judgment or her abilities. She had felt that Mamá still considered her just a child. But now Mamá was actually letting her make this important decision for herself! She was willing to let Cecilia leave the farm to follow her dreams. Was Mamá starting to recognize that Cecilia was growing up? Cecilia felt a warm glow of pride and satisfaction and a great tenderness for her mother.

"I will think about it then," Cecilia said. She gave Tía Sara a hug and, lost in her thoughts, went outside again to pump water for the kitchen.

Chapter 9

THE SHRILL CROWING of a rooster woke Cecilia up on the day of the wedding. She threw back the covers and jumped out of bed. Today was Tía Sara's wedding day! Mamá was already fixing Tía Sara's hair and arranging the lacy *mantilla* on her head. Over the *mantilla* she placed a traditional *corona de azahar*, a crown of wax orange blossoms. Cecilia put on her own new dress and felt like a princess. She helped Belia get ready and went to check on the boys. There was so much to do!

Tío Ben drove the bride to the Iglesia de San Isidro along with Tía María and Mamá. Everyone else, including Belle and Clory, rode in Papá's wagon. Cecilia rode up front with Papá so she wouldn't dirty her dress. After all, she was Tía Sara's *madrina*. When they arrived at the church, everyone went inside except Tía Sara, Papá and Cecilia. Edmundo was waiting at the altar with Elías, who was his *padrino*. Elías felt very important to be carrying the bride's gold wedding band in his pocket.

Cecilia walked down the aisle first. People in the pews turned to admire the pretty young girl with flowers in her hair. She carried a bouquet of spring flowers from Mamá's garden. She smiled at Edmundo and Elías waiting so seriously at the altar. She didn't feel nervous at all. When she reached the front pew, she stopped and turned to watch Papá escort her aunt down the aisle. All the people rose to their feet in honor of the bride. Cecilia thought she had never seen Tía Sara look so beautiful. Papá put Tía Sara's hand into

Edmundo's hand, and then he stood next to Mamá. Cecilia saw Papá and Mamá smile at each other. *They are probably remembering their own wedding,* Cecilia thought.

The wedding mass was long and filled with tradition. Padre Arteta asked the groom, "How are you going to support your wife?" Edmundo pulled out the traditional 13 gold coins from his pocket and showed them to the priest. He then placed *las arras* into the bride's cupped hands. *Las arras* are the gift of coins by the husband to his wife, which represent all his worldly goods. By this offering, he shows that he trusts her to take care of his household.

As the bride and groom knelt on satin pillows and spoke their vows, Cecilia and Elías arranged the *lazo* around their shoulders. The *lazo* was a white braided cord knotted in the shape of a figure eight. One loop was placed over Tía Sara, the other loop over Edmundo. "I unite you in marriage," said Padre Arteta. Then he blessed them and made the sign of the cross over their heads.

As the bride and groom left the church, they were greeted by a gun salute. The men outside the church began to fire their guns into the air, and the boys began to shout and yell. The ladies and girls threw rice at the happy couple. The bride and groom chose to walk back to the farm on the beautiful spring day. Everyone followed in a joyous wedding procession to celebrate with the couple at Cecilia's house. Jeep and Chata led the way carrying baskets of flowers in their mouths. Belia had spent weeks teaching the two little dogs this trick.

Edmundo and the men stood outside on the porch smoking and toasting with whiskey. Inside, the women were cooking a feast of *chile rojo con carne, frijoles,* baked chicken, rice, macaroni with cheese, tortillas, and many other tasty dishes. Everyone said the *bizcochitos* were delicious, and they admired the wedding cake Mamá had baked. The white cake was topped with the same cake decoration that had been on Mamá's own wedding cake. A tiny bride and groom stood under a wedding bell, surrounded by leaves and flowers. The entire decoration was made of sugar.

After everyone had eaten their fill, Papá pulled out his guitar and played a wedding song called *Los Recién Casados* in honor of the newlyweds.

> *"Ya llegó el día y el momento dichoso*
> *Que dos amantes se acaban de enlazar.*
> *Le dió su mano a su querido esposo*
> *Y con sus padres se puso a llorar.*

> *"Adiós mi padre, mi madre querida.*
> *Adiós mis hermanos y hermanas en unión.*
> *Adiós mis parientes y todos mis amigos.*
> *Sólo de ustedes espero bendición."*

> "The day and fortunate moment have arrived
> When two lovers have just been united.
> She gave her hand to her beloved husband
> And with her parents she began to cry."

"Goodbye my father, my dear mother.

Goodbye my brothers and sisters together.

Goodbye my family and all my friends.

I only hope to receive your blessing."

When Papá finished, everyone had tears in their eyes and the ladies cried into their handkerchiefs. Cecilia knew Tía Sara must love Edmundo very much to be able to leave her family behind.

Cecilia helped Tía Sara change into her traveling clothes. She and Edmundo would be driving to El Paso in his car. Cecilia carefully folded the wedding dress and *mantilla*. Perhaps she would wear them herself someday.

"Cecilia, I want you to have these. They belonged to my mother, your *abuelita* Eusebia," Tía Sara said. She handed Cecilia a tiny cup and saucer made of delicate china hand-painted with pink roses. Cecilia knew the cup and saucer were among her aunt's most prized possessions.

"*Gracias, Tía.* I will treasure them always. Oh, Tía, I'm going to miss you so much!" Cecilia said and hugged her aunt tightly.

"I'll be back to visit soon," said Tía Sara. "And think about what I told you. Edmundo and I are looking forward to having you live with us. You will have your own bedroom and more time for your studies. I know you will like living in El Paso."

The bride and groom raced to their car followed by all the wedding guests. The children were shouting, the women were calling out blessings, and Jeep and Chata were barking with excitement. Edmundo helped Tía Sara into the car, and they drove off in a cloud of dust. Behind the car trailed tin cans tied to the bumper with string. The words *"Just Married"* were painted on the rear window. Elías and the other boys had been busy decorating the car while the others were enjoying the singing.

That night the old adobe farmhouse seemed a little empty and lonely. Everyone was already missing Tía Sara. To make matters worse, Fito and Roberto, along with some of the other boys, had spent the afternoon collecting cigarette butts the men had tossed on the ground. While everyone's attention was on the wedding festivities, the boys had sneaked behind the barn and used the little bits of tobacco from the cigarette butts to roll cigarettes out of catalog paper. They had smoked them and made themselves sick. Fito and Roberto had confessed to Mamá because their stomachs hurt.

"¡Qué muchachitos traviesos!" Mamá said. "You are always getting into mischief! Well, you are lucky tonight. I am too tired to look for the *chicote.*" She fixed them a tea of *chuchupate*, an herb for stomachaches. Then she wrapped a long piece of cloth around their waists and tied a big knot at their stomachs to ease the pain.

The exhausted family sat on the porch enjoying the cool night air. Tomorrow everyone would share in the cleaning of the house. But right now they wanted to relax and talk about the day's events. *Didn't Tía Sara look beautiful? Wasn't the cake delicious? Weren't the dogs adorable? I'm hungry, are there any bizcochitos left?*

Cecilia sat in Tía Sara's empty chair. She listened to the crickets chirping in the garden. The frogs were croaking in the canal across the road. Otherwise, the night was quiet and still. Elías and Papá strummed their guitars. Mamá cradled Celia in her arms, while Belia sat with little Sylvia in Cecilia's old spot and leaned her head against Mamá's knees as Cecilia used to do. Fito and Roberto sat quietly for once, holding their arms around their stomachs. Cecilia smiled at her brothers. They were always up to something. She would miss all this if she went away to live with her aunt. A *dicho* she had heard somewhere crept into her mind: *A casa de tu tía, mas no cada día.* Visit your aunt, but not every day. Suddenly she sat straight up in her chair. She couldn't go live with Tía Sara in the city! How could she leave Papá and Elías and the boys? How could she leave Belia and Sylvia and the new baby? How could she leave Mamá? Mamá needed her here more than ever. This was her home! She belonged here! All her confusion melted away, and she knew what her decision would be.

"I'm going in to bed now," Cecilia said. She leaned down to kiss Papá on his cheek, and then she turned to Mamá. She put her arms around Mamá's neck and kissed her. *"Buenas noches, Mamá,"* she said.

"Buenas noches, hija. Que Dios te bendiga," Mamá said softly. "Sleep well, and thank you for helping with the wedding."

Cecilia went to her room. She lit a kerosene lamp and sat down at her dresser—the dresser Papá had made for her when she was twelve. She thought about the past year and all the changes it had brought. It made her head reel. So many changes! One upheaval after another. That's how life would always be. And she looked forward to all the changes that would happen to her in the future. But for now, she needed to be home—her own home with her own family. She had time to grow up. There was no reason to hurry. There would be time enough for all she wanted to do, for all she dreamed of. Right now she needed to be a sister. She needed to be a daughter.

Perhaps she and Mamá would never see eye to eye. Perhaps they would always have their differences. It didn't matter. What mattered was they were a family and they loved each other. There would be plenty of time later to play other roles, to be other things to other people.

Cecilia looked at herself in the mirror. She saw a strange new girl looking back at her—a young woman with a firm jaw and confident eyes.

"This is who I am," she said softly to her reflection. "This is who I want to be."

CHAPTER 10

Adonde el corazón se inclina, el pie camina.
Where the heart leads, the foot follows.

Querida amiga, guess what? I'm coming back to Derry in June! My *abuelita* is much better now, and my aunt is coming from Arizona to live with her. That means Mamá, Cleofas, and I can go back to our farm. Papá is happy we're coming back. He is tired of making the long trip to El Paso to visit us.

I've really missed all my friends in Derry this year. I liked my school here, but it just isn't the same. I miss the farm and my horse. I miss the fields and all the open spaces where Elías and I ride our horses.

I am looking forward to going to high school in Hatch next year. Just think—we will be sophomores!

I am sorry I did not write sooner, but I warned you that I am not very good at writing letters. When school starts, will you show me around the school? Do you think we can eat our lunches together under the trees like we planned last year?

I think about you all the time. I have missed you most of all.

Tu amigo, Johnny

AUTHOR'S NOTE

Cecilia Gonzales is a real person who really did grow up on a farm in Derry, New Mexico. Cecilia's dream was to get an education and to make a better life for herself and her family. Through determination and hard work, she was able to see this dream come true.

Cecilia graduated as salutatorian from Hatch Union High School in Hatch, New Mexico in 1938. Against her mother's strong protestations, she left the family farm for El Paso, Texas, where she attended the International Business College. She paid her tuition and supported herself through secretarial work, including working for the well-known architects, Trost and Trost. During World War II, Cecilia worked for the Office of Alien Registration under the Department of Justice and for the Post Quartermaster at Fort Bliss, Texas. Because she was bilingual, she was hired by the U. S. Office of Censorship, where she monitored telephone calls between El Paso and Latin America during the war.

In 1943, Cecilia left El Paso for New York City to marry her husband, Anees Abraham, a native El Pasoan. He had joined the army and was stationed in Pennsylvania. They were married for 49 years until his death in 1992. While in New York, she worked for the American Red Cross, where she met Mayor La Guardia and First Lady Eleanor Roosevelt.

In 1964, Cecilia became one of the first employees of the Chamizal Project under the U. S. Boundary and Water Commission. She served as a hostess during the transfer of the Chamizal to Mexico where she met President Lyndon B. Johnson of the United States and President Díaz Ordaz of Mexico. In 1967, she was the first employee of the Chamizal National Memorial in El Paso, Texas. She met First Ladies Rosalynn Carter of the U. S. and Sra. Carmen Romano López Portillo of Mexico during their visit in 1977.

Cecilia was assigned to take inventory of the LBJ Ranch home in Johnson City, Texas, before it was donated to the National Park Service by Mrs. Lyndon B. Johnson in 1968. Mrs. Johnson graciously met with Cecilia and the other Park Service employees, serving them coffee and cookies.

Besides meeting two Presidents and four First Ladies and retiring after over 20 years of government service, Cecilia has traveled all over the world to places such as South America, Europe, Greece, Turkey, Canada, the Caribbean, and Mexico— not bad for a young farm girl who used to sit daydreaming under a cottonwood tree.

*Saber refranes poco cuesta
y mucho vale.*
To know proverbs costs little
and is of great value.

Hay que bailar al son que le toca.
One must dance to the tune that is played.

Entre lo dicho y lo hecho, hay un gran trecho.
Between saying and doing, there is a large distance.

Más vale algo que nada.
Something is worth more than nothing.

Cuando no hay remedio, hay que adaptarse.
When there is no remedy, one must adapt oneself.

Tras la tempestad viene la calma.
After the storm comes the calm.

Más vale pan duro que ninguno.
Hard bread is better than none.

Abrazos y besos no rompen huesos.
Hugs and kisses don't break bones.

Dios tarda pero nunca olvida.
God may be late, but he never forgets.

No juzgues el hombre por su vestido;
Dios hizo el uno, el sastre el otro.

Do not judge a man by his clothing;
God made one, the tailor the other.

Panza llena, corazón contento.
Full stomach, contented heart.

Mi casa es su casa.
My house is your house.

Más vale poco y bueno que mucho y malo.
It is better to have a little of a good thing
than a lot of a bad one.

Si escupes para arriba, te va a caer en la cara.
If you spit in the air, it will fall on your face.

En la casa llena, pronto se cena.
In a full house, supper is soon ready.

Para olvidar un querer, tres meses de no ver.
To forget a love, go three months without seeing him or her.

Quien bien te quiere te hará llorar.
The one who loves you well will make you cry.

Si tú lo puedes imaginar, tú lo puedes alcanzar.
If you can imagine it, you can achieve it.

Bueno es cilantro, pero no tanto.
Cilantro is good—but not too much.

Caras vemos, corazones no sabemos.
Faces we see, hearts we don't know.

Nadie se acuerda de Santa Bárbara hasta que truena.
No one remembers Saint Barbara until it thunders.

Dios da y Dios quita.
God gives and God takes away.

Cada cabeza es un mundo.
Every mind is a world.

Mejor se guarda lo que con trabajo se gana.
It is best to save what is earned by working.

En abril, aguas mil.
In April, a thousand rains.

Cuando hace viento, quédate adentro.
When it is windy, stay inside.

Ya llegó por quién lloraba.
The one you cried for has arrived.

Del plato a la boca se cae la sopa.

From the plate to the mouth the soup falls.

Amor, salud, y pesetas, y tiempo para gozarlas.

Love, health, and wealth, and time to enjoy them.

Días de más, días de menos.

Days of more, days of less.

A casa de tu tía, mas no cada día.

Go to your aunt's house, but not every day.

Adonde el corazón se inclina, el pie camina.

Where the heart leads, the foot follows.

Other Great Books for Young Adults from Cinco Puntos Press

Cecilia's Year,
by Susan and Denise
Gonzales Abraham

Double Crossing, by Eve Tal

*Home is Everything / Home es Todo:
The Latino Baseball Story*,
photographs by José Luis Villegas;
bilingual text by Marcos Bretón

Sammy and Juliana in Hollywood,
by Benjamin Alire Sáenz

*Six Kinds of Sky:
A Collection of Short Fiction*,
by Luis Alberto Urrea

Vatos, photographs by José Galvez;
poem by Luis Alberto Urrea

*Walking the Choctaw Road:
Stories from Red People Memory*,
by Tim Tingle

DISCARD

DISCARD